THE
SCULLERY MAID'S
SALVATION

Emma Hardwick

COPYRIGHT

BOOK CARD

Other books by Emma Hardwick

CONTENTS

1

TEN BOB FOR TOFFEE

Elijah Sheehan was a runt of a man. His skinny frame was only five feet, seven inches. His bright blue, humour-filled eyes and broad smile belied the cruelty that lay beneath it. The angular face with its bony features was framed by a thick mop of prematurely grey hair, his skin snowy-white, devoid of colour.

Elijah had no character whatsoever. He stood for nothing, and he believed in nothing.

> "Aah," he would say to his cronies," I am a
> member of the Roman Catholic Church. You
> have to admit it, lads, they are the wealthiest
> church in the world."

Then, he would smile wickedly because he believed it was a status symbol to be associated with such riches. There was nothing spiritual or religious about him. He adapted his moral code depending on what was just about socially acceptable to the lower classes at the time, sometimes less than that. He was amoral. On his moral compass, true north did not exist.

Elijah was born in Belfast, Ireland, to Kel and Cookie Sheehan.

> "Well, Cookie my darling, we will just have to look after the wee one when he, or she, arrives," said Kel when Cookie discovered that she was pregnant for the fourth time.

Kel was a hardworking man who, eventually, had to feed seven hungry children and a wife. Upright, kind, and generous, he worked in a factory that produced iron components for ships built in the Irish shipyards.

> "Cookie," he used to say," It's time we left this country and went to a sunnier place. How come we are always cold in our own house? We will catch our death here."

Cookie was pregnant for seven consecutive years until she was too exhausted to perform her marital obligations every night. She was a good wife, and mother, she was house proud, and her children were educated to read, write, and count.

> "Oh, dear Gawd," she would lament. "Let them all just be out of the house, they do me head in."

The Sheehan family were considered in the upper echelons of the lower class by their peers, and even if they lived in a poor area of Belfast, they were well respected amongst their own. Their house had three bedrooms that comfortably housed their four sons and three daughters. Elijah's grandfather lived with them and was a bottle washer at an ale company. The old man's long coat pockets always held a treat for the small Elijah.

"Elijah, me lad. Look in me coat—ye may be lucky!"

The boy would feel around the pocket and pull out a sweet, and the older, and younger Sheehan's would sit, and chat with each other. It was a small treat in an otherwise harsh existence. Every day bled into the next, and little changed for years. Eventually, Elijah's growing feet began to itch.

"I'm struggling to look for a job, Da'. I am goin' to take meself to England."

At fifteen years of age, ambition drove Elijah south, over the Irish Sea to the great city of London which promised work, and prosperity. Such was his charm that he quickly managed to persuade a company to accept him as a carpentry apprentice.

"I am sound in me head, Mr Henshaw. Ye won't be sorry ye employed me," announced an enthusiastic Elijah

John Henshaw was taken in by the eager young Irishman. It was seldom one found a worker with such passion, and the talent to accompany it.

Elijah got his first taste of money in his wage packet, which he immediately invested in the Blue Parrot. He would often drink a whole week's pay until he was legless, but thought nothing of it—there would be more money coming in the following Friday.

Liking his grog, he loved the sensation of the smoky-gold liquid sliding down his throat, and the warmth, calm, and comfort that would soon settle over him. If only he could have stopped after a few drinks, Elijah, and the bottle could have had a healthy relationship, but it never did. He never saw himself as a drunk but, when he was plastered, he looked like a sick circus clown, mouth open wide, head lolling from side to side, and his eyes rolling in their sockets.

It was at this stage of his drunken journey that he would become antagonistic, argumentative, and finally violent. He said he had no memory of his behaviour, but that wasn't true. It was just a way to avoid responsibility for trashing the bar or beating someone half to death.

Elijah was by no means lazy or untalented, but as his taste grew for the brew, he struggled more and more to remain sober enough to do his work. Towards the end of his tenure with Mr Henshaw, days would go by without him showing his face when he had to. The young Irish man rented a room the size of a closet in the house of Mrs Trevayn on Upper Leeds Street. He used the privies outside and bathed in an enamel bowl. The bed had a metal cot frame with a coir mattress, covered by faded blue-striped ticking. Although he lived frugally, he did splurge some money on clothes, basic ones for work and a going out set. He chose to 'invest' the money his family gave him to see him off on his adventure. Going for a gander up town, he had got himself the most fashionable greatcoat and shoes that he could afford. He strutted around like a lord in his posh attire. He felt they were worth the expense. Every time he put them on he felt invincible—especially with the ladies.

He was a firm believer that first impressions are lasting impressions, and he wanted to be noticed wherever he went. Everybody saw him as an above-average smart young man on the road to success, but nothing could have been further from the truth. Elijah was a chameleon who changed his colours depending on whom he was with. He was adept at believing his own lies, and enough of a sociopath to get what he wanted out of anybody. Truth be told, Elijah was mad as a box of frogs.

When he was eighteen, he met Sally Bowman, three years his junior. A small lass who could give anyone a vicious tonguing with her shrewd mind. She wasn't ugly, just plain. Her light brown hair fell about her face like drab curtains, out from which peered a pair of nondescript, dull eyes.

Sally was illiterate and came from a family of eleven siblings. Her parents had given up trying to nurture them properly by the third child. The kids that followed were left to fend for themselves, with the older ones optimistically expected to step in.

At any given time, Davy and Susan Bowman didn't know where most of their children were. But that was how the slums worked. You were born into it and survived it— until you died of murder, disease, exhaustion or starvation.

Sally had realised her value at the age of nine. Lying that he was busting for the loo, her cousin of fourteen had asked her to walk down a narrow street with him late one Friday night and be on lookout. Chatting away, they continued to walk. It was a warm summer night, so they took a detour home through the scrap yard.

"Do you want some money for sweets, Sal?
Toffee, perhaps? That's yer favourite, ain't it?"
asked her cousin.

"O'course!" she nodded, delighted that someone was taking an interest in her.

He unbuttoned his trousers, and the fabric fell down around his knees.

"Touch it! Deal?" he said, with a cheeky grin,
then looking down.

Sally obliged his request, quite happy with her ten bob. What he asked was a little strange, but it didn't hurt, and she didn't feel violated. To be honest, it barely felt like 'work'. After all, the Bowman's lodgings were cramped, and they had all seen each other in various stages of undress. Privacy was not something that Sally was used to, nor particularly bothered about.

By fifteen, Sally could fulfil most needs, and she felt nothing—no guilt, no shame, no defilement, no anger. It was just her body doing what it did, and no one had ever told her not to. And as she got older, she enjoyed it.

Elijah was a master of lies and manipulation, so they made a good pair.

They met at the Blue Parrot one Friday night. Elijah was about halfway through his regular routine when she came to the bar asking for a whisky. Elijah was standing with his elbow on the bar counter. He thought it made him look grown up, like the older men from the dockyard.

"I'll buy ya one, angel," he chipped in, smiling at her.

"Why thank you, Sir. You are a true gent!" Sally replied.

"One for the lady," he quipped to the barman, thinking he sounded sophisticated.

"Where you be working then?" she asked, not really interested.

It was the first of his many lies to Sally. Elijah told her that he owned his own woodworking workshop.

"I am not spinning ya a yarn, darlin'," he smiled down at her.

Being a gal of little intellect, she was satisfied to accept his word as gospel, and he was confident that she was impressed by his little fib. He began to name drop and told her that he had professional relationships with some of the legitimate local businessmen in the area, men of good standing. Sally seemed non-plussed, so Elijah tried a different tack. He impressed her more when he mentioned his connections to the underworld, intimating that his relationship with some of the crime bosses bordered upon friendship, brotherhood even. He said that his influence and resources stretched far and wide, and he was climbing the ladder, all the way to the top, with the 'right' people supporting him, rung for rung.

"In time, me lass, I will be up there with the big boys! As sure as eggs is eggs!"

He raised his arm towards the ceiling and his gaze followed along with it, towards a mythical starry future. Sally's eyes did the same. Of all the lies he told, being the wife of a crime boss appealed to fifteen-year-old Sally's power-hungry suffocated psyche the most.

She sat and fantasized about the kudos she would have, if she were Sheehan's girl. In her mind, she could imagine Elijah giving orders to his sneaky sidekicks; where to go, what to steal, who to kill. She turned Elijah from an average, inconsequential, eighteen-year-old boy into a powerful man in the blink of her deluded, starry eyes. *We will have the biggest house on the street.*

People will shut their gobs when they see us. Folks will show us some respect when we walk about town. We'll be slum royalty. And I will influence Elijah, be the power behind the throne.

They went back to his window-less cell of a room. Mr Trevayn didn't care who Elijah brought home or what they did as long as they were quiet. All the times Elijah had previously been with a woman he had to pay, so getting it for nothing meant an extra few rounds at the boozer tomorrow. He did the calculation while he took off his trousers. It had cost him peanuts in drinks. He was going to get a bargain. Sally undressed, and the first thing she said was:

"What ya want?"

Elijah hadn't been asked that before. The regular five-shilling fee he usually paid for girls didn't buy him much choice. For the price of a couple of gins, he enjoyed the most depraved hour that he had ever experienced in his life, and he loved it. Sally participated physically, often leading the way with the most popular carnal skills she'd learned thus far. He tried his luck, and his imaginative suggestions were not knocked back. They went through the motions—several times and several ways. However, there was no sensuality or tenderness. They were like two animals, both satisfied, but there was no connection. Elijah was too narcissistic to consider how she felt, and Sally was too emotionally paralysed to ever be able to develop feelings for anybody. Nevertheless, they continued to meet.

Within a month she was pregnant. They made their way to the magistrate's office on foot, Sally hadn't bothered to even wash, and her stringy brown hair stuck to her cheeks. Elijah was still drunk from the night before, but since he was wearing his fancy coat, and snazzy shoes, he felt dashing.

The clerk of the court was not bothered at all by what stood before him. They were just another knocked-up pair from the dregs of society. Every day, Mr Morsdale rued his decision to go into public service. The two who stood before him were, in his opinion, irredeemably retarded, and now they were going to bring another feckless soul into the world.

The clerk had them sign the documents. He was surprised that Elijah could write his name. Sally could not, so she made a ragged-looking cross. Then Mr Morsdale dutifully forged the witnesses and the parent's signatures. He knew there would be no recourse for what he was doing. Nobody cared, and neither did he.

Sally was so painfully thin that it would be a surprise if she survived childbirth, and he wasn't convinced the child would survive either—if the state of the mother was anything to go by.

2

DRINKS FOR ALL, JOE!

They went straight to Davy and Susan Bowman's house to announce the nuptials. Sally's parents were sitting outside the back door on the step, trying to catch the last rays of summer sunlight. They were each holding a small glass, and on the ground before them, was a half-empty green bottle. Elijah got straight to the point. He was a married man now and wanted to exercise his new-found authority.

"We were married at the office t'day!" he proclaimed in his loudest, most outgoing manner.

"When is the bairn due then?" asked Davy with a sigh.

"June o'course!" growled Sally indignantly. "Can't ya count to nine then, Da'?"

"—nine months? Pull the other one, Sally! Let's not talk on the bloody steps, you lot," announced Susan, rolling her eyes with disdain. "Do you want the whole wretched row to know our business?"

"I can't believe you have got our Sally in the family way," grizzled Davy to Elijah as the small group melted away from sight.

"Ah, bloody hell, Davy, catch yerself on, will ya? If it weren't me, it woulda been another fella. Lucky for you I wanted to marry her, eh?" the newly-wed chortled, adding a cocky nod, wink and rough slap on the back, which irritated Davy enormously.

Nobody had ever stuck it to her Da', and Sally was impressed with Elijah's track record so far. The conversation drove a wedge between Sally and her parents that within weeks would widen into an unpassable gulf.

Wanting to celebrate their nuptials with friends, the couple walked arm in arm to the Blue Parrot. It wasn't a purely social call, of course. It was an excellent excuse for another bout of heavy drinking.

"One day, I am going to buy you a beautiful gold ring, my love," whispered Elijah in her ear as he squeezed her hand.

"Aww, what a lovely thought," cooed Sally, not really expecting anything to materialise.

It was the closest they ever came to having a romantic conversation.

"Me and Mrs Sheehan here—we're dying of thirst!" boasted the young Irishman to the Blue Parrot regulars.

A bawdy roar filled the room, followed by lots of back-slapping and lewd comments about the consummation presumed for later that evening. His mates had the capacity to celebrate any occasion if they could drink for free, and Elijah paid for the first two rounds to get the party started. He saw the initial outlay as a shrewd investment, hoping it would loosen them up so he didn't have to buy any more. There were speeches and jokes until the money ran out in the early hours of Saturday morning.

"Hey, Joe!" Elijah called to the barman. "Mind if we put another few rounds on the slate? I'll see you right on Friday, Joe? Promise!"

"Sorry, Elijah. How many more times? You know the guvna, Johnny, won't run a tab. It's time to take the misses home now mate. You're a married man now," the barman winked at Elijah.

"Look 'ere, son," protested Elijah, "I've spent a bloody fortune in here tonight."

"Sorry, mate. It's not for me to say. I just do what I'm told."

"Wind yerrr neck innn, Joe," mumbled Elijah in drunken outrage, his eyes rolling about his eye sockets, unable to speak properly.

"Don't you worry now, my love, I'll look after you," clucked Sally. "Yer missus will get more drink into yer belly!"

She looked across the bar with a flirty grin.

"Go on, Joe! Give my husband here a drink. I'm good for it," she purred as she fished about for a few coins then slapped them on the bar.

Joe poured Elijah another whisky shot. Sally pushed the glass gleefully into her intoxicated husband's fumbling numb hand.

"There you go, petal! You tuck into that!"

He gave her a drunken smile, followed by a slobbery kiss, then planned to drink until he almost collapsed. It turned out he wasn't very good at assessing the exact amount of liquor required, and soon he slipped into booze-fuelled unconsciousness.

Sally hadn't noticed. She was too busy singing and dancing her heart out, barely able to stand herself, let alone hold a tune. She looked across to her husband, keen for him to join in with the fun, but was disappointed to see him sparko in the corner of the pub. *It's time for a bit of fun for me then.*

Sally sauntered over to a group of men playing cards, putting out the word that she did favours. Two men followed her out of the back door of the pub into the alley. She leaned against the wall and lifted her skirt. One man followed the next, both watching each other's performance and both shoving payment into her bodice afterwards. In Sally's mind, she needed the money, and she couldn't get any more pregnant, could she?

She pulled down her skirt and went back to the bar, her cashflow problem solved. She bought another drink for Elijah, putting it in front of him as a nice treat for when he came round, and two well-earned gins for herself.

"Now, that's the kind of missus I want," said one of the men from the alleyway.

The others around him laughed loudly. Sally gave them a wink to suggest that further 'conjugal' rights were available whenever they wanted them.

She threw numerous drinks back one after the next. At first, she was dancing and singing, in full-on celebration. As the revelry and excess caught up with her, inevitably, her body slumped forward. She passed out, head on the table, thin, limp arms dangling down next to her body.

Joe the barman was so sick of drunks that he was ready to throw a complete wobbler. He shoved the boozy men out the door and locked up. He hid what bottles he could from behind the bar, not that it really mattered too much with the two patrons remaining. Sally was now on the floor unconscious, so too was her husband, a few feet away. As Joe walked past a comatose Elijah, he gave him a sharp jab in the ribs with his foot. There was no response. With a frustrated sigh, Joe went to his room upstairs, slamming the door behind him, knowing the sorry excuse of a man would still be there in the morning, along with his new wife.

3

SO, YOU'RE LETTING ME GO?

Baby Ebba was a miracle, born perfectly formed, despite the odds against her. Sally had a surprisingly easy labour. The under-nourished sixteen-year-old bore the child within three hours. Granted, she was too drunk to push the baby out of her womb effectively but Scully, the midwife, was experienced, and miraculously delivered the little girl into her new world.

Mrs Grantham, the neighbour, assisted the midwife. She took the tiny yelling bundle and looked down at her. The new little person was so small, and yet so loud. The scene made Mrs Grantham smile.

"Good job," she said to the midwife," God bless you! Nobody else could have done this."

"What will we call her?" Mrs Grantham asked Scully.

"Well, what does the new mum say?" answered Scully in a friendly tone.

"Never mind that! There's plenty of time to come up with a name. Right now, I need another drink!" yapped Sally. "I've got a throat on me."

The two women ignored her crass and thoughtless comment.

"I used to nurse with a lovely lass," said Scully to Mrs Grantham. "Her name was Ebba. It's German. I was told it means 'strong'."

"I like that," said Mrs Grantham with a big smile. "Sally, let us call her Ebba."

"If yer like!" muttered Sally sarcastically, stretching her neck to see if she could see a bottle anywhere in the room.

"Sally, you need to feed the little 'un," said Mrs Grantham gently.

She put the baby girl on Sally's breast, and she suckled hungrily.

"Ouch! That hurts! How bloody long does it have to hang on me bubbies?" asked Sally crudely.

Scully shook her head in disgust, and Mrs Grantham had to subdue her own urge to slap the insolent girl in the face.

"I will watch the child is safe, Scully," she told the midwife. "You go now. I will see you in the morning."

When Elijah finally made it home after midnight, he collapsed onto the bed next to Sally, unaware that there was a baby next to him.

Elijah woke up to an unfamiliar noise the next morning—the sound of his daughter crying.

He moved the blanket and saw little Ebba. Of everything he had to face today, this was the last thing that he expected or wanted. He nudged Sally to wake up. She had heard the crying but had done her best to ignore it for as long as she could.

"Make it stop howling," he complained to Sally.
"Me head is killing me."

Sally rolled over, pulled down the neck of her nightdress, and shoved her stinging nipple in the tot's mouth. Initially, it refused, which annoyed the young mother, keen to silence the thing, but a few more rough shoves later, the baby complied.

"Bloody hell, Eli! I can't take bloody much more of this. The pain is killing me. Pour us a drink, will ya?"

Elijah stood up fully clothed. Getting undressed in his drunken state last night was too much of a challenge. He stumbled about, then picked up two dirty glasses, and filled them with rum. He brought them across, along with the bottle. They both threw down three shots in quick succession. In a short while, the world started to look a little better.

Elijah made no effort to look or even touch the baby. He did not ask if it was a boy or girl or what its name was. However, he did consider himself 'cock of the block', and he wouldn't deprive himself of celebrating the birth of his child with the lads. It was another fortuitous reason to go on the lash. His mates had to show him the respect due to him on the occasion. So, he left Sally in bed with the baby, and what little was left in the bottle of rum, and made his way down to the Blue Parrot like any self-respecting new father would do.

Sally made a full recovery in two days. Scully, the midwife, sarcastically referred to her as 'a miracle of nature'. Elijah had not been back home since he had left for the Blue Parrot two nights ago. Bess Grantham was an angel, and she ensured that Ebba was fed, cleaned, and cared for.

Neither of the Sheehan's bothered registering the birth, despite the consequences if they were found out. With a bit of luck, the child would perish soon, and the loose end would be dealt with that way.

Bess had five daughters of her own, and the widow paid close attention to what was happening to her little neighbour. She went to check on Sally at least three times a day to make sure that the wee Ebba was getting sufficient sustenance, and being washed, and changed.

She tried to teach Sally how to boil water, and sterilise items which could prevent Ebba from getting ill, but a sullen Sally leaned against the wall and stared at her. With her selfish attitude, Bess thought the young girl could steal all the joy from even the happiest person's life. When Bess had finished with her demonstration, Sally handed over Ebba to Bess and promptly slammed the door behind her as she went down to the Blue Parrot. The loud bang startled the baby, and she started to scream her tiny lungs out yet again. A furious Bess, angered by Sally's self-interest, did her best to soothe the little thing.

Sally knew that she was dependent upon Bess. Usually, she did her best to behave appropriately in the woman's company. Still, it was not long before the young tearaway started leaving the baby with Bess for longer, and longer periods. Elijah had become so unreliable at work it was affecting Mr Henshaw. He could not run his business efficiently with Elijah's poor attendance record. Eventually, Mr Henshaw had no option but to give the skilled man the sack after yet another unplanned absence.

"How can you do this to me, Henshaw?" he yelled angrily. "For years, I have been your best carpenter! I have commitments now, a wife and child who depend on my wage to survive. You'll

have three workhouse deaths on your
conscience if you let me go!"

"I've given you more than enough chances,
Sheehan. You've let me down too many times. I
don't care how skilled you are. I have lost the
inclination to help you."

"Catch yerself on then, man!" raged Elijah.

Mr Henshaw had been in business for years and heard
every sob story that there was. He had seen Sally
Sheehan a short while back, and she looked like a victim
of the plague. She never had a bairn with her, and word
from the street said that she was always drunk. Elijah
screamed threats of violence at Mr Henshaw.
Eventually, the little runt was escorted off the premises
by two chaps twice his size both wielding hammers.

4

THE LITTLE GIRL NEXT DOOR

A slippery, sly fellow, Elijah Sheehan could turn any negative into a positive. In no time, he had Sally back on the streets earning their keep. To supplement the household income, he began fencing stolen goods. As his network grew, so did his head. He believed that this was a clear sign he was making progress in his life.

The career criminals, however, had no respect for Elijah. He was a show-off, with a loose tongue, and perpetually drunk. These were dangerous qualities in an industry that functioned on discretion. The goods that he fenced were small-time stuff, a piece of jewellery here, an ornament there, nothing of immense value like gold, art or diamonds. Most of what he handled were bits and pieces stolen by ragged little children picking pockets on the less prestigious side of town.

The baby was an annoying intrusion. He often had a desire to drop her at the poorhouse or sell her to a baby farm, but Bess Grantham kept an eye on Ebba and would have reported him to the authorities if she suddenly went missing.

Whenever he was at home, he forced Sally to feed the child because he could not stand the screaming of the hungry infant. This tension escalated the level of violence between the hapless couple.

"Sally, I'll kick you or that thing in the head if you don't shut it up."

Bess would often wake up to hear screaming, and cursing. She would open the door to their room, pick up the baby, and take her home. In the chaos, nobody knew that she had ever been there.

Sally and Elijah Sheehan drank incessantly in the years Bess lived next door to them. She had never seen either one of the couple sober. Without a proper job, Elijah always had a beer bottle in his hand. Sally drank gut-rotting gin all day, one shot glass after the next. Every time their door squeaked open, she could hear the light chink of empty bottles as they carried them back to the bottle exchange—and the heavy clank when they returned home with full ones.

At least Elijah had learned the child's name, even if he hated it.

"Ebba? Not a bloody Irish name that one, is it?" he had grunted.

Word had got around town that Sally was a wagtail and that Elijah was her pimp. Bess wished that they would simply get on with killing each other in one almighty row.

As Ebba grew, Bess began to feed her solid food and cow's milk. Bess could barely afford the expense, but she had good friends at the church, and everyone chipped in a bit toward milk for the little girl. She was glad Sally's erratic role in her care was diminished.

She was a joy to Bess, and her five daughters. They dressed her, bathed her, played with her, nurtured her. Ebba wore their hand-me-downs, but she was precious, and eventually spent all of her time in the Grantham's two-roomed flat.

"Oh, Ma, look at her! Bless her little heart, she is walking." said her eldest.

When Ebba began to talk, the family fell even more in love with her. Being with the joyous little infant worked her deep into their mutton. Thankfully, Bess received a pension from the government as her husband had been an army man. This managed to sustain her, and the girls. They did not live well, but at least, they survived without the constant dread of not being able to cover next week's rent.

The day that Sally and Elijah were suddenly evicted from their room was the worst day that Bess Grantham would ever experience. In contrast, the death of her husband was to be expected. He had caught a tropical disease when fighting in India, which had permanently weakened him. Bess had to nurse him for many months before he finally went to meet his maker. The swift removal of Ebba from the building was a painful loss all the Granthams felt.

In the weeks leading up to their eviction, Bess had pleaded with the girl's parents.

> "Please, Elijah, leave Ebba with me. I will look after her, you don't even have to pay me. We have helped her for years, now. What will she do without us? You said yourself she cramps your style."

Elijah was adamant that he would not hand the girl over. He didn't care what happened to the infant, but he did care about people thinking they could tell him what to do. Mrs Grantham as informed, in no uncertain terms, that she was an interfering old woman and had no right to tell him how to live his life.

It was the anxiety of not knowing her fate that Bess could not bear to think of. She tried another tack and met Sally on her own, begging her to relinquish Ebba, but she too refused.

Bess could never understand why they did not leave the little girl with her. It was clear neither parent had the faintest interest in her welfare, still seeing her as a burden, an embodiment of the unwelcome drain on their finances and impediment to their social lives. She dreaded the inevitable knock at the door signalling the child had finally perished. Bess could only pray for the girl. She had no right to take her on in the eyes of the law.

Eventually, the day came when the Grantham family had to say farewell to Ebba. For them, it was the same grief-stricken experience as burying a loved one. Sadness enveloped their little home, and it felt like all the joy evaporated. Everyone sat with a gloomy expression, looking at Mr Grantham's tarnished pocket watch on the mantlepiece. The agony worsened with each noisy tick-tock that filled the silent sitting room.

By the time three o'clock approached, every Grantham family member had their heart in their mouth. The wait was excruciating. Eventually, Bess had to give her daughters a talking to, else they would have sat in a circle sobbing.

> "Girls, we were given Ebba for a time, and that time has come to an end. God above has a far greater plan for her than you and I can understand. Watch and wait. Ebba will still achieve great things in her lifetime. I believe that with all my heart."

It did not ease the aching loss they felt, but the fresh perspective and optimism gave the children hope at least. Bess prayed that what she had said would come to pass.

There was a sharp rap of knuckles on the door. It was Sally. Bess handed the girl to her feckless mother, fighting to stop the tears running down her face. Ebba was giggling and bouncing about, thinking she was heading off on a big adventure, rather than a downward spiral. One by one, Bess Grantham's daughters kissed the child tenderly on the top of the head, then retreated into their room. The distraught girls overheard their mother ask Sally to visit them when she was settled, but she knew she would not see the youngster again.

Later in the afternoon, out on the landing, inevitably, they could hear two henchmen hammering on the Sheehan's door with their fists, bellowing that 'they knew they were in there.' Stubborn as always, the Sheehans were refusing to budge.

The news on the grapevine was that Elijah had not paid the rent for more than six weeks, spinning a few tales about them having 'a temporary cash-flow problem'. The landlord lost patience and had the young family forcibly removed by the courts. There were curses and threats wafting along the stairwell. All the residents in the building came out to watch the spectacle.

Sally shrieked and shouted like a petulant Shakespearean shrew. Scrawny little Elijah made violent threats he would not be able to physically achieve against the two big brutes at his front door. Had it not been so sad for the child, the fracas could have become the basis of a humorous sketch down at the music hall. Despite their wild protestations, their time was up, and the Sheehan's were frogmarched off the premises, their few possessions thrown out behind them.

For all of Elijah's supposed influence and connections with the underworld, in their hour of need, nobody would give them accommodation. Eventually, after a week of sleeping on the streets, as they augmented their savings with a bit of begging, pickpocketing and prostitution, the young family found a basement room in St Giles.

The space was small and crammed full with appalling furniture: a rickety bed, a shabby stove, two small chairs that creaked ominously every time they were used, and a table etched with deep knife marks. Black mildew was growing down the walls. The floor was permanently damp—water seeped up through the flagstones. The stench was so nauseating, they could have been living in a cesspit. There were no windows, and the room had to be permanently lit by candles. Elijah was too miserly, or stubborn, to provide money for oil lamps. Besides, he was never there. Sally was left in the gloom and spent her day sleeping or working for Elijah. Ebba was left to fend for herself.

Despite being very much down at heel, Elijah retrieved his ostentatious coat and shoes from the pawnshop. The trusty clothes made him feel good, despite the many hardships he faced elsewhere. Putting in place the final touches to his self-proclaimed dashing image with a trip to the public baths for a wash and brush up, he even found a lover. How a rogue like Elijah managed to charm Camilla Iverson into submission remained a mystery, but the beautiful and accomplished Camilla became obsessed with Sheehan. In bed, she teased him, describing him as her 'little bit of rough'. The Irishman, charming when he wanted to be, was strangely exotic and tempting forbidden fruit for a lady of Camilla's standing. He weaselled his way into her affections, flattering her, then exploited the relationship to the full.

She was a bored married woman whose husband owned a shipyard. Clifford Iverson was a respected man who professed undying love for his wife. From the day they met, her love-struck husband showered her with gifts, kindness and affection. She had borne him four prized sons and was the centre of his world. For the hardworking man, his family were the jewel in his eye. She, however, felt trapped, a desperately unfulfilled trophy wife.

Camilla felt she conducted the affair with the utmost discretion, so it was a devastating blow when her husband heard rumours of her reckless dalliance. Elijah, as always, never known for his subtle diplomacy wore his affair with Camilla like a new hat.

"Lads, I have found me a fine, fine filly," winked Elijah.

"Get away with ya!" laughed the blokes.

"Ooh yes, gentlemen. Best leg over I've ever had."

"A posh sort interested in a low-life paddy like you? I ain't 'eard nothin' like it! You have to pay five shillings to cop a feel down an alleyway with a bird, let alone have a free knee-trembler with a filly in a mansion!" joked his friend Jacky.

A furtive Elijah moved closer to the table and spoke in hushed tones:

"No, hear me out, boys! I ain't fibbin'. You know that smarmy Iverson git up at the shipyards?"

They all nodded.

"And that wife of his, Camilla?"

"We all know, Camilla!" Jack whistled, then grinned suggestively as he mimed the outline of an exaggerated hourglass figure with his grimy hands.

The men fell about laughing, and Elijah had to speak louder to be heard.

"Well, she's taken a shine to me, lads. Seems that man of hers can't make her happy—if you catch my drift. So, who do you know who might have the job now?" He paused for effect, then roared. "Me! I'm the man who's stepped up to the Iverson plate."

"We gotta have a round to that. You—Camilla Iverson's bit on the side. Who woulda thought it!" shouted Jacky. "Cheers, Elijah! Good on ya, mate."

Quite a few dockers were in the pub that day, and the rumour mill promptly went into overdrive.

Clifford Iverson, however, was a discreet man who loved his wife and wanted to forgive her, even if she had betrayed him with another man—a low life criminal to boot. Not a man who particularly cared about other people's opinions, he knew by not publicly acknowledging the affair, the gossips would soon move onto another target. He wanted to protect his sons to the best of his ability. Keen to limit the hurtful damage Camilla's careless, carnal wrecking ball had caused to his soul, Clifford bought her a beautiful flat in Mayfair. Then he swiftly divorced her, managing to pull some strings to stop the tabloids publishing it. Her generous endowment every month from him meant she became the mistress of her own destiny—an excellent situation for an independently-minded woman of the time to find herself in. Her friends secretly thought she might have picked up Sheehan to secure her personal freedom after pumping out all those babies for the Iverson dynasty.

5

THE COLD ALLEYWAY

By now, Sally had lost all her front teeth, and she looked more like a haggard forty-year-old. It was clear that she was not going to live to see her twenty-fifth birthday, let alone her fortieth.

Ebba was seven and severely neglected. She was the sweetest little thing, and again it was the kindness of a neighbour that rescued her from certain death. She often tripped over the child on the stairs or saw her playing outside with the other children. One day, Mrs Thomas chose to speak to her.

"Hello, wee lassie," she beamed. "What is your name then?"

"Ebba, Missus," answered the ragged little child. Her cheeks looked hollow rather than round she was so starved.

"Are you hungry, flower? Can I make yer some tea?"

A grateful Ebba nodded her head vigorously, about ten times in less than a second, Mrs Thomas counted.

The old widow took her back to her room and made a mug of strong, steaming tea with an extra spoonful of sugar.

"Thank you very much, Missus," chirped a delighted Ebba, tucking into the scalding hot liquid with relish.

Ebba gulped the tea down with such gusto that Mrs Thomas was amazed that she didn't burn her gullet. Then, the kindly woman offered her a piece of bread. Ebba was so hungry she swallowed it without chewing. Mrs Thomas was horrified. It was clear the child was starving, and something had to be done. An old maid who lived alone, she owned nothing but a bed, and a wood stove, and lived in a broom cupboard of a room. Despite her meagre resources, every night from then on, she shared her food with Ebba. Mrs Thomas was shrewd, and she did not want Elijah or Sally to know her involvement, so she told Ebba to keep their friendship a secret. The Sheehans were known for their violent streak, and she did not want to invite any more struggle into her life, or Ebba's.

Sally was pregnant again. It could have been anybody's child, but Elijah took the credit for being the only man in the slum potent enough to knock up his wife— a woman he gladly shared with every other man in the area.

By now Camilla had unceremoniously evicted Elijah out of her life. The relationship was teetering on the edge of destruction for quite some time, and collapsed once Elijah's careless blabbing had led to her unexpected relocation to Mayfair. Whilst she had 'landed on her feet' after the move and secured her freedom, there was no way that she would allow Elijah access into her new exclusive set. She moved to her grand new flat without giving Elijah notification of her address. She felt it was a nice neat solution to a problem that had grown monstrously ugly.

For Elijah, the pregnancy was all Sally's fault, of course. *How dare she get pregnant. Or more specifically, why did she stay pregnant? Why did she not get an abortion when she found out?* When Elijah brought the matter up, the exchange resulted in a severe beating for Sally. It was a miracle that she or the seven-month-old foetus survived. The other vaguely bright thing in the bleakness of the Sheehan's situation was that Ebba was utterly oblivious of the violence.

"Ebba!" called Mrs Thomas seeing the girl playing in the courtyard and heading towards the entrance to the tenement. "Come take a walk with me to the shop. I need to fetch a few things. I need help carrying it. Quickly, girl. I haven't got all day!"

The hastily engineered excuse provided an escape from them hearing Elijah trying his best to kill Sally. Yet again, Elijah was drunk. His vicious, cruel streak resurfaced. Mercilessly, he raped her. His 'angel's' eyes were now beaten closed, and her bruised lips swollen and shiny, like rings of black pudding.

Ebba slept at Mrs Thomas's that night, but nobody at the Sheehan's noticed. For the first time in years, Sally was sober because she was too injured to walk or drink. Elijah had practically skipped with glee to the Blue Parrot. He bragged to the lads of how he had clobbered Sally good and proper and slammed back shot after shot, eagerly toasting his achievement. Hours later, he had started a fight with a stranger for a bit more late-night devilry. He was given a good hiding and lost both of his front teeth. Blood oozed from his mouth and nose. He held his tender ribs and limped home, but collapsed some distance from it. The depraved Elijah Sheehan had got what he deserved.

Sally worked the streets up until the contractions made her clock off. Again, against all the odds, she gave birth on the filthy blood-soaked mattress with the help of a midwife whose income was mostly earned by terminating pregnancies rather than delivering babies. Elijah insisted on naming the boy Kelsey after his father.

"This little cherub will have me dear ol' pa's name, a decent bloody Irish one, no more Kraut nonsense," he yelled in his drunken stupor.

The basement was still bare and cold, and the pitiful coal stove fighting a losing battle to heat it. If the Sheehan's situation when Ebba was born was dire, it was now hopeless. Now mid-winter, sewage seeped up through the floor, and the room flooded every time it rained. They were ankle-deep in a mixture of run-off water, faeces, and soot. Life revolved around living in a freezing square of brick, sleeping on a blood-stained mattress with no food to eat.

Little Kel screamed and screamed from constant hunger. Ebba tried her best to soothe him but to no avail. There was no Mrs Grantham, and Kel was too small to eat proper food. Sally could provide almost no milk due to both a lack of sustenance and interest. She would lie unconscious for hours on end with Kel next to her. Fuelled by his strong survival instinct to stave off starvation, exhausted and neglected, her son would still fight to reattach to her breast, desperate to drain what little he could from his mother.

Elijah was mostly absent. Sally preferred it that way. All meals were based on a loaf of bread because there were no utensils to cook with. When Sally finally regained consciousness, she would get up, and stagger to the door on the hunt for some drinks and bunk-ups against the boozer wall to pay for it. Ebba would be left with Kel.

Mrs Thomas was the second angel who would be a saviour to the Sheehans. She decided to boil up some marrow bones then set them aside to cool for a while. *Surely the stock from the bones and marrow was light enough for Kel to swallow.* Then, she ladled some of the liquid into a small bottle, and fixed a rubber teat she found to the top. The plan was to sustain the boy until she could contact the parish guardians. She knew that the perilous situation the Sheehan children found themselves in could not continue any longer. She had to alert the authorities and soon. If she failed to do that, she would have the death of two innocent little children on her conscience.

Knowing that the good-for-nothing parents would not return until the next morning, she cleaned up Ebba and Kel as best she could. Then she took the babe in the crook of her arm. She offered him the teat, pushing it against his lips, praying he would accept it. To her relief, after considerable insistence on her part, he did. Ebba would get a chunk of crusty bread and a tiny piece of cheese mushed up with some marrow water. Mrs Thomas was so afraid of Elijah that she would sneak the children back to the basement, cover them both as best she could then disappear like a ghost. The elderly woman who had almost nothing for herself was a saviour of two children who had even less.

Sally died on the streets. It was just like any other occasion when she drank until she collapsed, but this time, it was a bitter midwinter's night. The streets were glazed with dirty black snow that had turned deathly cold as the temperature dropped. She had been at the Blue Parrot all evening. A few punters had used her in the alley, and Sally was so drunk after drinking the proceeds that after the last man, she couldn't get to her feet. She lost consciousness out on the cobbles in the icy slush. Joe, the barman, found her in the alley when he closed up in the early hours. She had frozen to death.

6

THE IMPOVERISHED SAVIOUR

Little Ebba, although not so little now, was seven years old, and her brother Kel was almost one. Mrs Thomas loved the two children as if they were her own. They had given a purpose to her long lonely days. Elijah knew that she looked after them during the day but would not acknowledge her efforts because she may have asked for payment.

Mrs Thomas tucked them up as warmly as she could, then she boiled some water, and put it into ceramic bottles. It got their temperature up just a little.

"Come, me little sweethearts," she would smile. "Let's get yer all cuddled, and cosy, there. Ebba, put yer little arm around Kel. Snuggle up to your sister, that's right, lad," she cooed as the little boy grinned at her, his eyes twinkling with affection.

The heat dissipated quickly, but it helped. Little Kel seldom cried. For Mrs Thomas it was quite a miracle to have satisfied the tot against all the odds. She had grown fond of the lad and loved nothing more than rocking him in her arms, looking down at his face brimming with glee. It was summertime, but the basement remained damp, and cold all year round. She had requested a meeting with the parish guardians, although it would take a while to get an appointment. The Sheehan children simply could not stay in the basement any longer. It was not fit for rats, and they needed to be taken somewhere else. It broke the woman's heart. She had a limited income from her daughter, and the children were growing. Soon, they were going to need more help than she could provide.

When Elijah bothered to come home, he slept in the same bed as the youngsters. He always arrived in the early hours of the morning reeking of alcohol. Ebba hated being close to him. He would breathe his stinking breath over her, and snore with his mouth open, revealing his toothless blackened gums. He was unaware of anything around him. Ebba was, however. She could not bear the man touching her, so she would put Kel between them.

Elijah opened the door to their basement lodgings, cursing loudly at the water flowing down the steps, flooding the squalid room below. His voice wafted down the stairway.

"I'm sick of this hell hole! Ebba, will ye clean it tomorrow?"

Now, a sour mixture of alcohol, body odour, and women overtook the room's damp, sewage-laden smell. He was talking loudly to someone no one else could see. He tripped on a flagstone before falling down awkwardly on all fours with a nasty thud, protecting his drink bottle more than himself. Oblivious to everything around him, he collapsed onto the bed. Making sure nothing spilt from the bottle that he was carrying, painstakingly, he lowered it onto the floor next to him, ensuring it would be within reach on waking. Ebba shut her eyes tightly, pretending to be asleep. She could smell the stench of the man, and the stench of the room. It sickened her.

Ebba woke up unaware of the exact hour because there were no windows to provide a clue, but surprisingly, she felt well-rested. A tiny chink of sunshine bounced through the gap between the door and its poorly-fitting frame, just enough to penetrate the gloom. Kel was still asleep. He usually woke up because he was hungry, but he seemed fine today. Ebba was thankful for that. Elijah lay an arm's length from her, mouth open, breathing his toxic breath over the baby. Kel was sleeping so serenely that she just watched her precious little brother for a while. His tiny hand was poking out from under the blanket, almost like he was waving. At first, she was charmed by it, but on closer inspection, his fingers seemed blue from cold. She touched his hand; he felt chilly. She lifted the blanket to put his cold little limb under it, but she couldn't move it. She sat straight up, her hair hanging down the sides of her face. She nudged him, desperate to wake the lad up, but he was stiff. In Elijah's drunken sleep, he had rolled on the child during the night and suffocated him. Ebba understood death. Everybody in the slum understood it. The reaper was never far away, lurking malevolently in the dark corners, ready to pounce. She knew her brother was gone, and in a mix of loneliness, grief and terror, her lungful of air came out as a piercing scream.

"Shut yer pie hole, child! Can't you see I'm trying to sleep?" shouted Elijah, but she couldn't. She was seven years old in a room with a monster and her dead brother; she was filled with panic.

Her first instinct was to get away, to run as far, and fast as she could. She went to Mrs Thomas, but she was not in her room. Ebba's little mind was overwhelmed. She could not bring herself to go back to the room and didn't want to be out alone, either. She ran down the few steps by the front door of the building, still screaming hysterically.

The sun was surprisingly high in the sky, and it was warm. She had to put her hand over her eyes until they grew accustomed to the light. Not knowing where to go or what to do, she walked for two hours, her little body exhausted and famished. Eventually, she sat on the pavement, traumatised and bewildered. Deciding she needed to go back to Mrs Thomas, she headed in what she hoped was the right direction. She wandered around for hours until she finally admitted to herself that she was lost. She sat on the kerb and sobbed, grimy black streaks running down her face, nails dirty, and her whole body stinking.

Ebba saw a water pump down the road and walked towards it. She gave two hard pulls, and water spurted out. She drank until her thirst was quenched and the edge was taken off her hunger, then returned to the spot where she had been sitting. It was outside a factory, and there was a small recess in the wall just big enough for an adult to fit into. The only downfall was that there was a grate where she had to sit. She slumped down on the thick steel grille, a literal fly on the wall. Nobody noticed her, but she saw everything.

Feeling the toasty air rising through the grate from the factory, it warmed her as the sunlight faded. Starving but too tired to hunt for food, the lonely little lass fell asleep sitting up, her soft face touching the rough brick wall.

Waking up with a fearful sensation that someone was standing over her, at first, she panicked thinking it was Elijah. Moments later, as she felt the walls around her, everything came flooding back. Ebba looked up to see there was indeed a person watching her intently, nudging her roughly with their foot, but it wasn't her father.

"You are in my spot," hissed the voice.

She could not make out the face clearly. It was too dark. Not knowing what to say, she stood up and prepared to run for it. The person picked up on her nervous body language.

"Hang on a minute, little miss. What is your name?"

She identified a boy's voice.

"Ebba."

"So, you're a girl, are ya?" he surmised with a faint giggle.

There was a kindness to his tone, and Ebba let her guard down a fraction.

"Yep. What's your name?"

"Simon Long, just call me Simon," the boy announced. "Are you hungry, Ebba?"

"Starving," she said, adding, "I ain't eaten nuffin for ages, days."

"Well, here you go then," he smiled as he broke his piece of bread in half.

He pulled a bag from under his coat and opened it. He took out an apple. Ebba had never seen an apple before. They shared the fruit bite for bite. It was the most divine thing Ebba had ever tasted, and she told him so.

"Where did you get it? Ya didn't steal it did ya?" she asked him.

"No, silly. A kind lady gave it to me after I swept her chimney," answered Simon with a chuckle.

Ebba took a better look at him. With all the soot, she could not identify the colour of his hair that clung to his scalp. Raggedly dressed, he was a little bit bigger than her. She guessed they were about the same age. She stared at his pitch-black face and a big pair of mischievous, blue eyes.

"How come you're dossing here then? Don't you have a mother and father?" enquired Simon.

"My mother and brother are dead, and I hate my father. Too fond of using his fists when he's been on the sauce," she answered honestly.

"My ma has a new husband, and he beats me black and blue for the fun of it. So, I prefer to live here," explained Simon, gazing at the tiny alcove.

"I have to be back at work soon, else I'll get a clip round the ear off my master, for being late. We got another rush job on tonight." he grumbled. "This is a good spot to sleep. That warm air warms the cockles of your heart," he added, tapping the metal grate with the toe of his boot. "I found it by accident. Tell you what, Ebba. I will share the space with you. While I'm at work, you be on guard and make sure nobody else takes it, then we swap?"

"How am I supposed to keep people out here on my own?" she asked.

"Cor, blimey! It's simple, innit! You sit there and scream bloody blue murder if someone tries to move you on. Do I have to teach you everything?" he tutted, gently teasing her.

The lonely seven-year-old girl laughed out loud. For the first time in a long time, she felt joy.

Ebba and Simon lived happily in their little corner of the world. The warm air blowing through the grate kept them cosy at night. Ebba made sure nobody took their spot. Simon shared his food with his new companion. Their hygiene was appalling, only being able to wash under the pump when they forced themselves. It was pointless, anyway. Having only one set of clothes, they perpetually stank. Most days, their faces could not be seen for the dirt.

Elijah considered the death of little Kel more of an opportunity than a bereavement. Taking the deceased infant to the hospital, he made a few pounds out of the tiny corpse, selling it as a highly-prized fresh cadaver to the medical school. With infant mortality rampant in the slum, no one seemed to care about the child's sad demise. In his grubby mitts, joyously he toyed with the cash payment and went, forthwith, to the Blue Parrot. Pretending he needed rallying through his grief with his boozy chums' support, he was roaring drunk by ten o'clock that evening.

To appease her concern, the old lady, Mrs Thomas, had tried to get some information out of Elijah regarding Ebba's whereabouts. He fobbed her off with a sob story, telling her he was too grief-stricken to discuss the matter. He didn't want to waste time debating the brat with his bloody nosey neighbour.

Sally's death set him back financially, and he wanted—needed—to make some easy cash. The horrid little man already had his eye out for a few girls he could pimp, but they had to have qualities that would best serve him. Ideally, he looked for the destitute and desperate, especially those addicted to a substance of sorts, whether laudanum, opium or alcohol. He did not care which.

7

THE SNOWY STREETS OF LONDON

Ebba had turned eight. She was completely unaware of the date or the significance. It was a cold, brisk autumn day, and the bone-chilling wind was channelled through the depressing streets. It was the sort of gale strong enough to keep the ships sheltering in the harbour. Finding food and staying warm was becoming more of a challenge. The channel of warm air that escaped up through the grate helped, but as soon as Ebba stepped out of the little alcove, she would freeze all over again. It was challenging to find clean water to drink because the pumps froze up in the cold. The nook had an overhang which protected them from the rain, but as carriages passed by water was splashed on them. To insulate themselves, they put newspaper around their bodies, and then put on as many garments as they could find. Simon found an unforgiving piece of rough tarpaulin on the scrapheap near one of the houses he had swept. It was small, but Ebba and Simon rejoiced at the find. The canvas was about five feet square, but it was a godsend, providing welcome respite from the wind and rain. They guarded it with their life.

The two children pressed themselves together and shared the tarpaulin. Even though the rain might stream down the street, and the wind howl, they were sheltered in the alcove, with its small overhang above and the warm air below. Simon promised that he was saving some money to buy her some new shoes. Her feet were growing, albeit slowly, and the one pair she had pinched terribly. They wouldn't be strictly 'new' shoes, of course, and would likely be third or fourth hand with some patched holes, but they would be better than nothing.

Simon was having difficulty providing enough food because it was winter. The 'easy food' was challenging to find. He could no longer pick an apple hanging over a garden wall. Bread or cheese required money. Barely able to look after himself, now he was worrying about Ebba too. They snuggled up to each other as best they could. Most nights, it was hopeless. Trying to sleep sat up with their knees under their chins was desperately uncomfortable. They had to contend with the constant ache of maintaining their contorted sitting positions, hunger or cold—usually all three. It was still better than being alone, though.

Simon taught Ebba how to warm bricks at the street fires where the homeless would gather. He was friends with a toothless old woman called Ada who put each of theirs by the flames, then handed them back, wrapped in rags, so they didn't burn. The youngsters would tuck the covered bricks under their clothes with relish. The warmth would flood through their bodies. The idea was brilliant.

The greatest challenge in making fires was finding fuel to keep them going. Ada's sole purpose each day was to walk street to street collecting pieces of coal that may have fallen off a coal truck. There were many like her.

For the first time in many seasons, January brought snow. The white fluff was startlingly beautiful, and Ebba watched it drift in the air, fascinated by the powdery flakes that settled upon the ground. It did not remain white for very long. The thick smog from the belching chimneys drifted down upon it, making it a horrible sludgy grey-black. But for an instant, a few minutes, the white snow gave the impression that the effluent-filled streets were clean and fresh. It was a moment of magic in the middle of the mire of filth.

One evening, Simon did not come home. Ebba panicked about what could have happened to him. Hungry and frightened, with reluctance she went to find Ada, breaking the golden rule of never leaving the alcove unattended. She had not eaten since the previous night, so she took their precious rag-covered bricks and walked down to Ada's street fire. At least she could be warm if not fed. The orange glow from the dancing flames caused long flickering shadows to rise up the sides of the building. The whiter patches of snow took on a warm colour, but the air remained bitterly cold. Someone in Ada's street family had brought a bottle of grog, and they were passing it around the circle. The drink was warming them, and amid all the hardship, there was laughter and friendship.

A raucous hub-bub from the many bawdy conversations taking place broke the evening silence. Ebba squeezed in between the towering adults, and then crawled down at their feet to get closer to the heat. Nobody paid any attention to the small child. She was adept at being invisible. It was a useful skill she had honed years ago to avoid a beating from her drunken father. Eventually, she tugged on Ada's ragged skirt.

"What is it, lass?" she mumbled with her toothless mouth.

"Ada. It's Simon. He ain't back yet. It's not like him—" Ebba snivelled as she started to cry.

"Sit there by the fire, Ebba. Warm yourself up, eh? You'll catch yer death. He'll be around fast enough. You'll see."

As she smiled, her smooth wet gums and greasy greying hair glinted in the firelight. In any other circumstances, it would have been a frightening sight, as if one of the undead were stalking the earth. That night for Ebba, however, the vision was a godsend. Staring down towards the base of the soothing fire, she just saw a pair of pitch-black shoes push into the circle.

She looked up the length of the body until she saw the face of Billy Rhodes. Simon worked for Billy. Billy was a tall, distinctive fellow, with grey hair down to his shoulders. His top hat was crinkled, shabby. His old-fashioned tailed coat had no buttons on it.

"Hey, Billy!" bellowed a voice. "It's late! You got a nice bottle of grog in those lucky coat pockets of yours? It'll warm my poor ole bones a treat!"

"I'm not stopping long," replied Billy, dodging answering the question.

"What you eating tonight, then? Give it here. I'll take the chill off it," offered the kindly old woman.

"Nowt, Ada, my love. Ain't got nuffin to heat through tonight. Only stopped by for a free warm," came his resigned reply.

"Had a bad day then, Billy-o?" asked a different voice, a woman's.

"Yeah, no bleedin' work got done," answered Billy.

"Why not? Got less business 'cos of this 'ere snow?" the voice continued.

"Nah, me wee sweep got stuck, and we couldn't get him out the chimney for ages. Took all day to rescue him. The lady of the house fair went mad.

Wrote off the whole day. Didn't even pay us for the work." announced Billy, dismally.

"Oh no, that's awful. Still, tomorrow's another day. If he rests up he'll be ok." another woman quipped, trying to lighten the mood.

"The wee lad was—was a good 'un." Billy lamented, not really paying attention to the chit-chat.

"Was? So, he's no more, then? That's terrible. Who was the lad the Good Lord took for himself, Billy?"

"Wee Simon Long. Smothered he was. It were terrible. Heard him struggling, fighting fer breath and then—"

Billy's voiced failed him for a moment.

"Oh no, Billy," cried Ada," Not Simon! He was a little angel," she whimpered.

"He was me best boy. The son I never had—I suppose. I hate this bloody business. Aye, he was a good 'un. Looked after his little urchin friend too. Name of Ella, was it? Something like that. I dunno where the lass is. I am dreading telling her."

"Here! Here, Billy. This is the gal, not Ella, but Ebba!"

Ada pointed a bony finger towards the girl as she stood up. But, rather than approach Billy, she turned and pushed her way through the lofty adults once more and fled without looking back.

"Come back, Ebba! Come back," screamed Ada.
"You'll surely die of cold! Come back."

A few people lumbered after her, but on the slippy surface, the nimble little youngster was too far ahead. She turned a corner, then another. The slum was a cramped maze of streets, and soon she had disappeared. It would be impossible to find her.

Ebba's breathing was laboured, the smog-laden, cold air burning her lungs. She pushed on regardless through the snow-covered lanes, the holes in her tatty shoes soaking up the icy water like little bilge pumps. Freezing cold, she felt no self-pity, only exhausted hopelessness. A lamp flickered here, and there, chimneys puffed smoke, but there was not one door that she could knock on for help. In St Giles, it was everyone for themselves.

Eventually, she could run no more. She collapsed on a quiet street corner, and sat there in a heap, without any desire to move. The lane was dark, with high brick walls all around her. There were no stars or moon just pretty snowflakes fluttering down from the blackness above.

Soon the cold overcame her and she began to feel an uncontrollable drowsiness. Everything around her seemed to drift further and further away. She closed her eyes, just to rest for a little while. A moment later, the darkness overcame her fully, and the pain from the cold was gone.

In the rapidly worsening weather, a flurry of flakes descended upon the little girl and gently enveloped her. Within minutes, the beautiful pure white covering was greying, polluted with soot from the factory chimneys. Soon, Ebba Sheehan's body was just another snow-covered bump in the road.

8

THE BOY RUNNING THE ERRAND

Elliot Chadwick was gasping so heavily that vast plumes of white air were billowing from his mouth every time he exhaled. He was wearing a brown newspaper boy cap pulled as low as possible. Wrapped up in a greatcoat with a thick black scarf swathing most of his face, he knew it was wrong to run on the treacherous ice, but he was cold and he wanted to get back home to warm his bones. There was no traffic at that hour, so he didn't think it mattered too much if he slipped over. Late for an errand for his mum, Jess, who ran the coffin house, he rocketed down the middle of the roads, smoothing off the corners to his route. Almost home, forgetting to focus on his footing, he hit something solid, and he went careering through the air, landing in the snow which was not as soft as it looked.

He got back to his feet slowly, remembering the street was slippery. Usually, he would have stood up and moved on, but his instincts and curiosity compelled him to go over to the small bump to see what had caused him to tumble. It looked like a bundle of dirty old rags that probably fell off the back of a cart. Elliot was way too inquisitive for his own good, so he scraped the snow off the fabric, only to see the small face of a child.

For a few seconds, he was perplexed, with no clue if the child was dead or alive. He thought the right thing to do was to gather the girl in his arms and started running again. If she were alive, she would stand a better chance if she were inside, he reasoned. If she were dead, at least she would have some dignity.

The coffin house was the size of a warehouse. Wooden boxes the size of caskets were lined up row upon row. The place was busy, mostly full of men either sleeping in the coffins or lying on their sides, talking to each other. Some chaps were sitting on benches, their arms draped awkwardly over ropes in front of them, wrestling to get comfortable enough to perhaps have a few hours' sleep.

Each wooden box had a tarpaulin to stave off the cold, but thankfully the great room was warm. There were several colossal coal stoves placed at intervals along the walls, where water was boiled, and broth was warmed throughout the day, and night. Each end of the warehouse had a massive hearth, twice the height of a man and ten times as wide. Great coal fires burned within them, and the firelight reflecting on the red brick walls gave an impression of homeliness. The poor underdogs who stayed there were of all races, colours, and creeds with the same things in common: they were tired, homeless, and hungry.

The coffin house was close to where he found Ebba, and Elliot made it there in a few minutes. He opened a door in the arched entrance hall, running into the immense warehouse, dodging the protruding coffin ends as he went. He ran straight to an anteroom and saw a woman bandaging the head of an old man. Jess Chadwick was in her mid-thirties. She had wide eyes and good humour. Her brown hair was always tied in a knot behind her head, and she had a pretty face. She was often referred to as the fiercest woman in the Salvation Army, but she was really an angel in disguise. It was as if God had made her for the sole purpose of looking after vagrants and vagabonds. Every day she put on a spotless grey dress with a white apron, but by breakfast time, it looked like she had done a full day's work in it. She was quick with a smile and had an empathy for the men, and women she looked after. Although, she could also be stern, getting on the wrong side of Jess was difficult to do. If you did, however, there were severe consequences. She was never afraid to dole out a punishment when it was needed.

John, her husband, was business-like, and efficient. Whereas she was friendly and outgoing, he was more introverted: stoic, deeply religious, and disciplined. He had worked in the Salvation Army for ten years, and he knew that it was his calling in life. He wore the uniform proudly, determined to be a beacon of hope, and kindness to the folk that he served. He never held himself above anybody else. His demeanour was the same towards the numerous wealthy benefactors as the lowliest paupers in his care. He represented his organisation with pride, having to integrate with all echelons of society to further the purpose of the Salvation Army or raise money for projects. He had a diplomatic manner and was adept at negotiating with difficult officials, and even was tasked by the organisation to present their cause at parliamentary committee meetings.

He succeeded in reaching his objectives where other's failed because he spoke from the heart, and he was never hooked into any political power play. His mandate was clear, and so was his conscience. John's word was law, and his wisdom was respected far, and wide. His staff of fifteen would, on any given night, provide food, and beds for two hundred people.

"Ma! Ma! There is a child here!" exclaimed Elliot. "She is frozen. I found her collapsed on the street. I don't know if the Lord has taken her already?"

"Give me the child!" Jess barked assertively.

The young matriarch marched off to the washrooms, skirts flapping behind her as she disappeared. Holding a mirror under the poor girl's nostrils, she looked for the faintest hint of fogging. There was nothing. She put her ear next to the girl's face and mercifully, she heard the tiniest hint of breath she was so desperate to find. The warmth of the building was working its magic.

Jess barked:

> "Walter, go fetch a bath and fill it with water—
> not too hot. Suzanna, bring a blanket and make
> tea with a lot of sugar in it."

Looking over at her maid, Jessica was unhappy with her efforts.

> "Hang on, Suzanna! More than that, girl!
> Honestly. She needs it sickly sweet! Quick as you
> can now. That's better!"

More orders came thick and fast.

> "Walter, get a screen up at the fire for crying out
> loud. I won't have all and sundry gawping at her
> when she's undressed."

Keen to find out more about the newest arrival to her premises, Jess turned to her son.

> "Elliot, where did you find her?"

> "A few streets away. I tripped over a lump when
> I was hoofing it over here. It was her—lying in
> the snow. She must have collapsed or
> somethin'."

> "Thank you. Now, get to the front of the house,
> Elliot, they need you there. Did you give Granny
> Palmer her medicine?"

"Yes, Ma," he answered diligently.

Elliot then reached into his pocket and fished out four pennies which he gave to his mother.

"What's this?" she asked.

"Four pennies, Ma," he said. "Please let her stay the night, and give her a plate of food."

"Good gracious, Elliot! Do you really think I'd send this poor little waif out because she has no money?" Jess shook her head and glared.

"Don't be so fierce, Ma. I was only asking to be polite! I didn't want to assume. You brought me up to be a good boy!" teased Elliot as he gave her a playful dig in the ribs.

"Alright. I'll take the money. What a good lad you are," she said, deciding to humour her son.

Jessica Chadwick put the for pennies in her pocket for safekeeping, planning to give them back to her son later as a surprise for his thoughtfulness.

Jess carried Ebba to the fireplace and got to work behind the screen. She took a pair of scissors and began to cut through the rags. By the time she got to Ebba's body, the smell was so terrible that she couldn't wait to put the lethargic child into the water and give her a good scrubbing with some carbolic soap.

Ebba was just conscious, but couldn't move on her own. Sleepy and dazed, she realised that a woman was removing all her clothing. She would have been forgiven for panicking in her vulnerable state. Thankfully, the glorious heat radiating onto her face and body let her know the efforts of the person were most likely for good, not evil. It was the most substantial hearth she had ever seen. The blazing fire burned enough to warm the whole warehouse, and thaw the shivering little girl. Her body, freed from the freezing rags, was transferred by Jess to a copper tub, the size of an enormous broth pot. The lukewarm water felt it was scalding her icy skin, and she cried out as soon as the immersion began.

> "You will stay in their child!" ordered Jess "Bring more water, Walter," she yelled over her shoulder. "And do try and remember the carbolic soap this time, or I'll be sending you off again."

Ebba had never taken a bath before, but the trauma of nearly freezing to death did not mar the experience. Sat shoulder-deep in the large copper tub, the warm water was now giving her the richest sense of wellbeing that she had ever experienced in her life.

> "Suzanna!" shouted Jess, "Where is that tea you were told to bring to me. It will be stone cold by now! Make a fresh one for the girl, and while you're there, make one for me as well. And for goodness sake, don't forget two sugars—"

Suzanna trundled off, muttering 'Yes, Ma'am!' as she rolled her eyes. *Wasn't it understandable I had forgotten the first brew as I was more concerned that the child was still alive?* She returned with the two mugs of tea as requested, handing them over promptly, to avoid another well-meant telling off.

"Watch her Suzanna, and scrub her down with that soap. She's so encrusted in dirt you could grow potatoes on her."

Suzanna gave Ebba the tea while she was still sitting in the tub. The drink was delicious and filled not only her stomach with warmth but her heart. The kindly maid gave the girl a minute to relax before the scrubbing would begin in earnest.

"And what might your name be then, Missy?"

"Ebba. Ebba Sheehan."

"Well, I am Suzanna, and I work for Jess," was the explanation given to the bewildered little face.

"Is that the fierce lady?" asked Ebba with big eyes.

"She is not so fierce, just—organised. She has to be," laughed Suzanna. "It's quite a task looking after all the people here. She's got a heart of gold though. You'll see."

Ebba smiled.

"Well, we better scrub you, and see what's underneath all that dirt, shall we?"

Once given the nod, Suzanna washed Ebba from head to toe. Walter was run ragged, bringing fresh warm water, and taking away the old. It took several rinses to clean her to the standard Jess would be expecting.

Suzanna laughed at Ebba when she refused to get out of the tub.

"Don't you want to get out of that water! You'll dissolve like that sugar in your tea!"

From the tub emerged a pretty little girl with a big smile.

Her hair was lovely and clean and dried quickly in front of the fire as she brushed it. Suzanna found her some clothes. They were a bit big for her, but they were clean and warm.

"Who is that boy who brought me here?" asked Ebba.

"Oh, that's Elliot Chadwick."

"How do you know him?" asked Ebba.

"Jess is his mother, and he helps out when he is not at school."

"School? Mrs Thomas said that only wealthy people can go to school."

"I am sure Jess will help with your education," Suzanna laughed. "Elliot wants to be a doctor."

Ebba smiled at her.

"I am going to be a nurse, Suzanna."

Jess appeared at the door.

"Please let Ebba sleep upstairs with you, Suzanna. I don't think it's good for her to stay down here with so many men about. You can't trust everyone."

"Right you are, Jess."

Ebba settled into her warm bed beside the maid. She was engulfed by a sense of wellbeing. She was clean, she had eaten, and she was in the care of kind people. Her last thought before she drifted off was of poor old Simon. How grateful she was that he had tended to her when Mrs Thomas no longer could.

9

THE WARMTH OF THE COFFIN HOUSE

"Suzanna! Walter! Come here please," yelled Jess at the top of her voice, which was nothing strange for her colleagues.

"Suzanna, where is wee Ebba, and how is she holding up?" she asked.

"She is doing well," laughed Suzanna," I believe she thinks she is in a hotel. She has been sorely neglected."

"Don't get too attached to her Suzanna, we may need to send her to one of our children's facilities," said Jess, ever the practical one. "You know it's difficult to keep children in this environment. Look out for her until we can make a better plan."

Jess Chadwick knew that she was preaching to herself as much as her staff. It was a lecture she had given so many times, and yet, she was always the one to break her own rule. That was how Suzanna and Walter had ended up at the coffin house as permanent staff.

She walked into her husband's office without knocking, then stood by his side, gently resting her hand on his shoulder, waiting until he was finished with his bit of paperwork.

The room had shelves from floor to ceiling, and they were filled with hundreds of ledgers, records, and books. Nobody would ever accuse John Chadwick of embezzlement.

He swivelled his old leather office chair around, and pulled her onto his lap. He was such a hard worker, and she was filled with admiration for her husband. She would watch him sitting at his roll-top desk, working late into the night, occasionally smoking his pipe as he pondered tricky issues.

"Jessica, you have a problem you need me to solve, don't you?" he whispered good-humouredly into her ear.

"You know me so well, John Chadwick," she laughed.

He pretended to be stern.

"Out with it then?" I don't have all day."

"There is a young girl—"

"—no, Jessica!" instructed John before she could go any further.

"But John, the child is about eight years old. I cannot send her to an orphanage or poorhouse," said Jess.

"You said that about Suzanna and Walter. Then you took in Kate, and Joanna, who are now in the kitchen. No, Jessica," said John, keen to lay down the law.

"But look at them now, my dear. They are corps cadets. We are training a new generation of highly capable Salvationists. How do you think we are supposed to grow as an organisation?"

John knew what Jess was saying was true. The force of charity needed new members of all generations.

"You can see that the lass has had a hard life. She has settled overnight, and to send her off into some God-forsaken institution will be like sending her back to the hell she came from. Look how well the others have done. Some of the children we kept have been educated, and have good lives today. Look at David McDonald. This is where he started. Now, he is a local officer with a wife and two sons. If we had not helped him, John, he would still be in the gutter—or worse, dead as a door nail."

"Jessica, you want to collect the needy like other people collect postage stamps. We agreed not to have lone children here. They are at risk if they are unaccompanied. You know that if it is a family, it is acceptable, but we cannot have one little girl amongst two hundred men."

"I promise we will oversee her welfare," begged Jess. "Please, John, I will find a place for her. I just need to think it through."

"So, you're looking to ignore the rules again, come what may," muttered John, closing his eyes, and shaking his head.

He had been through scenes like this so many times with his wife. The conversation always followed the same pattern. He would say no, and then he would give in, with her getting exactly what she wanted out of the situation.

"John, the staff like Ebba already—that's her name—and Suzanna suggested that Ebba can shadow her. But I am going to put her out of harm's way in the kitchen with Bunty. Winter is our busiest time of year. An extra pair of hands cleaning up the scullery will be a tremendous help. It will free up the more experienced staff to focus on meal provision."

"Suzanna is as bad as you are," said John without humour. "Yes, yes, yes. Alright. She can stay. Just keep her away from bother. Be warned, if I hear one word of trouble arising from this, she will have to go."

Jessica kissed him lightly on the forehead.

"Thank you, my darling. I love you all the more when you are feisty," she murmured in his ear.

"Humph," he groaned, with a faint grin.

Jessica left his office victorious, knowing that he always gave in to her if the reasoning was sound. John shook his head as he watched her go. He would do anything for her, and she knew it. In all the years he was married to Jess she had never complained about her lifestyle. Other wives would have wanted more conventional lives. Jess was an angel, and the coffin house could not run without her.

John had joined the Salvation Army in its formative years. He was a young man looking for a career where he could make a difference to society. Coming from a middle-class family, he was educated as well as his father could afford. He could choose any career that appealed to him, and he went through all his options with a fine-tooth comb.

Realising that he wanted to reach the core of people's happiness, he sought to reach their souls. John was a firm believer in the poor being treated with dignity. All most folk needed were people who cared enough to help lighten their load, and then they thrived. For the poor, living from hand to mouth, knowing that they could only afford to put shelter over their heads for the next few days, at best, was a living hell. Some people thought they were better off dead, and many did die—by the thousands.

The life of the poor was an assault on their body, minds, and souls, but if he could help these people feel worthy, then perhaps other people would see their worth as well. He wore his colours with pride, as did all the staff under his command, both the volunteers and the candidates in training.

John Chadwick was the commanding officer for the Greater London area. It was a position of power—and trust. Everybody within the organisation referred to John simply as 'Colonel'.

As a youth, he remembered he and his father disagreeing vehemently on his chosen profession.

> "I educated you to establish a career that can give you esteem in society, status, an opportunity to earn and income that will serve your family well. And yet—"

"Father, I do not begrudge other people their choices, and I do not judge either, but I choose to take this path."

"How did you even get involved with this loathsome institution?" asked his father insultingly.

"One day, I saw their marching band on the street and watched them preaching to the poor. They had a passion for what they were doing and a sincere sense of duty. They want to improve the lives of those poor unfortunates. A few Sundays later, I found out where their citadel was, and I attended a service." John explained.

"What is all this jargon? It sounds like a blasted cult," cursed his father.

"That is just how they refer to their structure, but the crux of this ministry is to uplift the East End of the city—"

Mr Chadwick could not bear to hear another word.

"—Just blunder on John. You have always had your head in the clouds. When your finances are in a parlous state, and you cannot look after your family, do not come begging to your mother or me."

John left the room disappointed with his father, a man who always preached charity and equality, yet did nothing to instigate change. He was compelled to continue, with or without his father's blessing, unable to turn his back on those most in need. It was the one thing that gave his life real purpose.

What appealed to John about the Salvation Army was that it did not discriminate. He had seen all nationalities and creeds shelter in his coffin house: Jewish families destitute from pogroms on route to their communities all over the world, Indian Sikhs miserably out of place in the British cold, former slaves, waiting for the next ship to return them to their homelands. The organisation catered for everybody, and if any Englishman dared to persecute a foreign man, John would evict him immediately.

The slogan in the slums for them was: 'Soup, Sleep, and Salvation'. A small collection of underappreciated people, they did their utmost to serve humanity in the most challenging of circumstances. Their real motto was very powerful: 'Blood and Fire'.

"Now, Suzanna, I don't want Ebba idle," advised Jess. "She can help Bunty in the kitchen. There is a lot to do there."

"Yes, I'll take her through."

"With the bad weather, all that snow on the streets, we are going to be overrun tonight," warned Jess, with a hint of gloom and determination.

"Walter!" she yelled. "Please speak to the lads in the coffin store, and see if they have any more they can put out for the night. Jones, the supervisor, will help rearrange everything."

Captain Jones sauntered up to Jess:

"Mrs Chadwick, we don't have space. Last night we were already over the limit for our headcount. Plus, our food rations won't stretch," he lamented, knowing it was of no use to suggest putting a limit on numbers, but proceeded anyway.

"Nobody will die of cold on our watch if we can help it, Jones. Smaller men can double up in coffins, top-to-toe. We will have enough soup, even if we have to eke it out with a bit more water. Let's get as many beds out there as possible."

Ebba stood and watched, staring wide-eyed. Never had she seen such a determined force for good as Jess before. Her mother had been determined, of course— but only to find another drink. She made a mental note to live up to Mrs Chadwick's expectations.

"Come, Ebba!" beckoned Suzanna. "Let me take you to the kitchen, and introduce you to Bunty. You'll like her."

They left the sleeping quarters and passed through another area in the vast warehouse. There were rows and rows of long tables and benches.

"What is this room used for, Suzanna?"

"This is the dining hall. With a squash, we often probably put five hundred people in here."

"Five hundred sounds like an awful lot!" announced an astonished Ebba, who struggled to count past ten—the most her fingers would allow.

"Bunty, over there, is the head cook and will find you a job to keep you busy. There are ten staff and volunteers in the kitchen preparing soup for tonight, peeling vegetables, washing dishes, baking bread. I will see you later on," explained Suzanna, gently pushing the girl by the shoulders in the cook's direction.

Bunty got Ebba working immediately.

"Come now, lass. We don't have time to hang around. Let me show you what you need to do."

Taking her to the scullery, she explained:

"This area is always getting dirty, so you are in charge of keeping it clean. Pick up all the crumbs that fall on the floor. We don't want any beasties moving in and feasting. Clear up any spills promptly so no one slips. Sweep, and wash the tiles twice a day. The mop and bucket are in the scullery. You are in sole charge of the kitchen floor. Do you understand? I want it spotless all day!"

The fair but commandeering tone in the chef's voice indicated that Ebba had better do what she was told.

"Yes, Bunty!" said an obedient Ebba.

The kitchen was an area of both magical merriment and significant stress. There was a constant flow of people and goods through it, and Ebba began to understand why Bunty was so obsessed with the floors.

As the delivery men staggered in with heavy overfilled boxes of fruit and vegetables, a few of the smaller items rolled off their piles. These would trickle under the dark crevices below shelves and cupboards. Chunks of bone and offal would slither off the butcher's carts and slap on the floor. Weighty sacks of flour were prone to puffing out white clouds of dust as they were thrust into the stores. The girl was kept busy. The sensation of the head cook's observant eyes boring a hole in her back as her contribution was assessed ensured that Ebba's productivity and efficiency remained high. When Bunty's beady eye caught an exhausted Ebba slumped, using the mop handle as a crutch to keep her tired body standing, she shouted across the room:

"Remember, the last things I want is rats and roaches in my kitchen. This will be the cleanest kitchen in London."

Ebba's day began at six. There was no set timetable for the crew in the kitchen. Breaks were squeezed in when there was a rare opportunity to do so, with the staff perching on stools by a large food preparation table, gulping down a snack. If Jess spotted a lull in her punishing workload, she would rush in for something to eat, then rush out again just as swiftly.

One afternoon, she shared a place at the table with Ebba.

"Hello, my flower! I haven't seen you to speak to for a while now. Has Bunty got you working hard?" smiled Jess.

"I think she is pleased with my efforts so far," replied the girl.

"You must be working hard, Ebba. This floor is spotless."

The girl smiled from ear to ear.

"Mrs Chadwick," said Ebba bravely. "I want to be a nurse."

"You do?"

"Yes, I want to help sick people. Make them well again."

"Why is that, then? What's brought this decision on, all of a sudden?" asked Jess, interested to hear the story that might emerge.

"Well, my best friend, Simon, died. And so did my little brother, Kel. Perhaps if I was a nurse, I could have saved them?" she answered, unbeknownst to her that she could have made no difference in either case.

"I am sorry to hear that, Ebba. Yes, we can all make a difference. But, to be a nurse, you need to go to school first."

Ebba looked at her and frowned, then her eyes were downcast, as though she realised the dream could not be.

"Ahh! Don't be downhearted sweetheart. There's always a way if you look hard enough. I tell you what—I am going to talk to Sergeant-Major Chadwick and see what he has to say about all this."

"Really? Do you think it could happen?"

"Yes," said Jess, ruffling the girl's hair affectionately. "I think there is every chance it can happen."

Jessica barged into John's office, giving him the fright of his life.

"Jessica!" he moaned. "You are going to give me a heart attack!"

"John, listen to this. I have an idea."

Jessica had countless good ideas each and every day without fail. He still couldn't figure out why she wanted to discuss them with him. The strong-willed woman had a mind of her own—and she usually got her way.

"What—or who is it now?" he asked.

"Young Ebba Sheehan."

"Yes, she can move in permanently. Yes, she can work here. Yes, we will look after her." John sighed.

"We're already doing all that for her," chuckled Jess as a fond, exasperated-look took residence on her husband's face. "This is something else."

"Please don't tell me you want to adopt the child, Jess?"

"No, my love," she giggled. "I want to send her to school. Give her a chance of having a better life. Earlier, she told me that she wants to be a nurse."

"Well, then enrol her at the school down the road. That will be a start. I do not promise any more than that, though. She is not our flesh and blood."

"Oh, thank you, my darling, I knew you would agree," smiled Jess as she darted off towards the door.

"Jessica, before you leave—when this child is old enough to study at medical school, she will have to live in the city. Do you have any idea about how you will bankroll this dream of yours? I will not be dipping my hand into my pocket. We are stretched enough as it is. Is that clear?"

"John, I know she is still very young, but she can always join the medical fellowship like Elliot did. We can raise it with the advisory committee. Mary McAlistair, one of our most generous benefactresses, has paid for the education of many young doctors to serve in the fellowship. I can't answer that now, but I know that when the time comes, there will be a solution. Ebba wants to be a nurse, not a doctor, so that makes it far less fraught—and cheaper."

As she closed the door behind her, John shook his head. He knew she would find a solution. She always did. Frowning at the papers in front of him, he tried to forget the interruption and get back to what he was supposed to focus on.

Ebba loved being in the kitchen, especially making new friends. She realised how vital camaraderie was to her wellbeing when Simon passed on. She was keen to fill the gap his death left.

"Ebba. Come here!" roared Jessica one morning.

Ebba was accustomed to Jess yelling like an irate general by now, and it didn't startle her like it did at first. With so much to manage, everyone knew Jess's reason for directness.

"Yes, Jess," answered Ebba.

"I have enrolled you at the Methodist Parish School down the street. You will start at nine in the morning, and be home by three in the afternoon."

"Are you going to come with me?" asked Ebba startled.

"Suzanna will take you, and fetch you every day. You will be safe. Bunty will pack you something to eat. When you come home, you will clean the kitchen as agreed. You might be a pupil, but you still need to earn your board and lodgings here if you are to continue to stay."

"But—but, why must I be away from the kitchen all day! I like it here!" protested the girl.

"Shush, child. You will still live with us," said Jess, firmly, not wanting any backchat from someone being given a leg up in life.

Ebba looked overwhelmed by this new change to her day-to-day living. Being separated from the kitchen staff would be a tremendous wrench. Jess continued explaining the plan she had for the girl.

"Did you, or did you not say that you want to be a nurse?"

"Yes, a nurse, Ma'am," she said shamefully, feeling the full weight of the reprimand for her ungrateful attitude bearing down on her.

"If you want to be a nurse, Ebba, you have to go to school. Do you understand that? Your parents may not have taken the slightest interest in your education, but that is not the case for Mr Chadwick and I. Nursing is a responsible job. People will depend upon you—to save their life perhaps. It is not a career to be chosen on a whim. You need to be highly trained. And that training begins with school tomorrow, my girl."

All the pieces of the puzzle began to arrange themselves in Ebba's mind, and she smiled at Jess.

"Now I understand," she answered with a delightful smile. She was no longer scared; she could not wait to get into the classroom.

10

HUNGRY MOUTHS TO FEED

"Bunty" yelled Jess, from the scullery," I think we are in for about two hundred mouths tonight, have the vegetables arrived yet?"

"Yes," said Bunty," and they are a good quality. Not wizened up like that last lot Mr Hendricks sent us."

"Bread? How is the baking going? I don't want men waiting till midnight to eat."

"All on time, Jess."

It was the same questions every day, and Bunty provided the same answers. As always, one of Jess's barked instructions followed another.

"Suzanna, it's time to fetch Ebba from school."

"Yes! On my way."

"And no dilly-dallying, please. She needs to come back to clean the scullery floor and do her homework."

Suzanna laughed.

After her chores, Ebba spent her evening doing her homework at the kitchen table. It doubled as the best writing desk in the public area of the coffin house. There was usually such a commotion that she was surprised Ebba learnt anything at all. Nevertheless, the girl's grades were excellent and she enjoyed the challenge that all her subjects provided.

Most of Ebba's conversations these days began with 'did you know—'.

Suzanna grabbed her official Salvation Army hat and walked down the road at a brisk pace. Even with the gloomy grey clouds, and black smog hovering menacingly above the slum's streets, it was summer, and pleasantly warm for an English day.

She wore her uniform with pride. The Salvation Army had immense local support, and with it real power to address social problems in the area. It was an organisation that was willing to do the dirty work to help in the slums. Working with the town councils to improve health and hygiene, they fought for the rights of downtrodden people, the voiceless in society. Everywhere Suzanna went, she was greeted with a polite 'Hello, Miss', and men doffed their caps when she passed.

Ebba was delighted to see Suzanna and began giving her a blow-by-blow account of everything she had learned that day on their way back. The comprehensive rundown only stopped when the girl bounced into the kitchen, like a ray of sunshine.

"Hello, Bunty! Jess!" she chirruped.

Jess smiled at her, pleased that the child was positively thriving these days.

"And, how was your day?" she enquired, using her softer, nurturing tone of voice.

"Oh, excellent, Jess. I beat Gerry Taylor at sums today. Did you know that he was the smartest pupil in the school till I beat him?" she laughed.

The delightful contagious giggle filled the room, and it continued as she jigged around the kitchen. Jess laughed too. She could not believe that the girl had been with them for five years now. Ebba was growing up to be a beautiful young lady, and Jess kept a beady eye on her. There were always opportunists after young girls, and Ebba made sure that she was constantly accompanied by a chaperone when out and about.

"I need to walk to school myself tomorrow— we're starting earlier, at eight o'clock. We have a guest speaker at half-past."

Jess's ears pricked up at the change of Ebba's regular routine.

"That sounds interesting. You and Suzanna will need to get up an hour earlier tomorrow, then."

"Can't I walk to school alone? I am thirteen, and I can look after myself."

Jess was disappointed to hear her ask with a whining, entitled tone to her voice, and nipped the idea in the bud.

"Absolutely not," cautioned Jess. "You are my responsibility. Either Walter walks you or Suzanna walks you. You never go anywhere alone. Do you understand me? And don't think I won't take a whip to you if you disobey me either."

"Yes, Ma'am," protested the girl as she slouched away to the other end of the kitchen.

Jess had never beaten her even when she perhaps deserved it. Still, Ebba knew that Jess meant business, and she decided it best not to disobey her, just in case.

Jessica climbed the steps to John's office and flew through the door like a hurricane.

"Good morning, Jess. Why you look so beautiful today. What do you want from me this time," he asked with a wink.

"I need a favour, John. When I say a 'favour', I really mean 'a big favour'."

"Go on—" he said, with a hint of trepidation.

"Ebba needs to study here in your office. Her homework is getting quite complicated. She keeps losing her train of thought with the constant distractions. The kitchen is in chaos at the best of times. The child needs to concentrate on what she is doing."

"Jessica, I can't believe that you are asking me this. This office is a place of business, not a school classroom."

"John, you have a library in here that is never used, books that are never read, and she can benefit from this."

"No, don't ask again. It is a firm no."

"This is what I was thinking," proposed an undeterred Jess. "There is a small annexe, next to the window, just enough space for a chair, desk, and lamp, and we will clean it up. John, you won't even see her, and she can work in peace."

John frowned. She was doing it again. His wife was making sense. *Really it would not be an imposition. The girl is a delight.* He was sure that if he gave Ebba a lecture on being quiet, and on how the library worked, she would leave him alone.

"Alright. But if I don't like having Ebba here, I am sending her back to the kitchen," grouched John not wanting to look like a pushover.

"Oh, thank you! A hundred times over! I knew that you would say yes."

She walked over and hugged him. Anybody ever tell you that you are the best husband in the entire world."

"Women wouldn't dare," he chortled. "They would be too afraid of you finding out!"

Jess left the room and laughed all the way to the kitchen.

Within a week of studying in her new environment, John and Ebba were firm friends. They had developed a daily routine. On her way down to the kitchen for breakfast, she would pop in, and say good morning to him. The large office was built on a mezzanine floor, and its windows looked out over the coffin house. John could watch everything that was happening. Ebba's desk was in a recess between two windows. She had promised Jess she wouldn't be a nuisance, and faithfully kept to her word.

The three other walls in John's office were lined with shelves that went up to the ceiling. Ebba needed a ladder to get to the books at the top. Returning from school just after three, she and John would have a brief discussion of what had happened that day, then they both got back to their books.

There was a small Dover coal stove in the corner, warming the room. At five o'clock it was tea time, and it was usually Walter who brought a tray of tea, and sandwiches to John's office. Ebba and John would eat together, and they would have a detailed conversation of what she was learning. Ebba was proficient in algebra, and science, and John was sure she would qualify to be a doctor, but he did not say anything. There were very few female doctors. Society still preferred women to be nurses.

That evening John, and Jessica lay in bed together. She was curled in the crook of his arm.

"You need a holiday," Jess suggested, stroking his neck lovingly.

"Not now," said John," We are preparing for this quarter's exams."

"What?" enquired Jess, clueless as to what the reply meant.

"Ebba and I are preparing for her midterm exams," replied John

"I thought you didn't want her bothering you," smiled Jess.

"Well, the things they are learning these days are exciting. I am getting a second education."

"She will be turning fourteen soon, John."

"Yes, one of these days she will have to choose a university," he replied.

Jess propped herself up with an elbow to look at him better, surprised by his answer.

"Yes, Jess, that girl is far too smart to be a nurse. She has the potential to become a doctor."

"Have you discussed it with her?"

"I will, of course, when I think the time is right. Let us get these first formal examination results, and then we can take a more informed view."

"Will we be able to get a bursary for her from Mrs McAlistair?" asked Jess.

"Yes, we stand a reasonable chance, I suppose."

Jess's practical, nurturing mind was on fire.

"She will have to board at the McAlistair home in Kensington, close to the University. How will we persuade Mary? Money is one thing, but a lodger, well this is something quite different."

"Jess, you are thinking too far ahead. Let's just take it a day at a time for now."

Jess kissed him. He pulled her closer. They had the same passion for each other as when they met. She loved him, and he adored her.

11

BACK TO THE BLUE PARROT

Elijah Sheehan found himself broke. Again. With nothing to his name, he had called in all the favours he had outstanding. Nothing was forthcoming. Downhearted, he badly needed a drink, so he decided to pay a visit to the Blue Parrot. It was only just noon. He treated the bartender to his old Irish charm, hoping to weaken his insistence to follow the landlord's tiresome credit ban.

"C'mon, Joe! How long have I been coming here? Just one drink, that's all I ask! Pop it on the slate, you know I'll be good for it."

"How many more times, Elijah. You know the rules mate, nothing for nothing."

Sheehan began to lose his temper. His mouth was turned down at the corners, and his eyes were narrow.

His demeanour irritated the barman. He was tired of people trying it on to get free booze.

"Lawd above, no!" bellowed Joe. "Go home, you potless Irishman."

With that, an enraged Elijah thumped his fist on the bar and gave a stark warning.

"All right. I hear yer. I'm going. But I'll be waiting for ya outside. Teach you a few manners about how to treat yer regulars!"

"Is that right, you ratbag?" taunted Joe. "Don't make me come over there! You'll get a lesson you won't forget in a hurry. Now—get out!"

Elijah knew that he had no chance against Joe, drunk or sober. He left the pub in disgrace, his plans for the drink he needed so desperately, thwarted.

It was clear to him, there was only one more person who could help. Camilla Iverson. The more he thought about her, the more he convinced himself that if he could find the woman, she would be only too happy to pay him lots of hush money. Weeks after she left the family home, he continued to brag about his carnal conquest of her in the Parrot. Some of the shipyard lads pulled him up about it a while ago. They knew he was lying because he had no idea she'd moved to the West End when quizzed. Still, the embarrassment was worth it. He had a fresh lead to follow about her whereabouts.

He started his walk toward Mayfair, which was a good few hours on foot. With every step, his rage and resentment grew. He was in a foul mood. His hands were shaking. He craved alcohol like a starving man would hanker for food. He wasn't very brave when he was sober and lost all sense of humour. Without his boozy, rose-tinted glasses, the drunken charisma he displayed in the bars of St Giles, turned into an ugly bitterness, fuelled by the harshness of reality.

After Clifford Iverson divorced Camilla, she disappeared into the gracious world of the upper classes. Elijah now planned to search for her, spending time walking the streets and parks of Mayfair, desperately looking for her. It occurred to him that he would stick out like a sore thumb and that he was way out of his depth. He had no chance of ever hobnobbing with the rich and famous.

In all honesty, Elijah had given up the thought of ever finding Camilla. However, now desperate for cash, he was determined to give it one last ditch attempt.

He decided to try Green Park, being one of the smallest in the area, a mere forty-seven acres. He felt helplessly out of place in his usual garb: his smelly coat and battered shoes. His usual clothes were pitch black from head to toe. Although he would have looked acceptable in St Giles, he looked like a dirty undertaker in the manicured gardens of Mayfair. The park was lush and green. People strolled or sat on park benches enjoying the sunny day. Elijah's beady eyes were peeled.

The small eatery was packed with wealthy people enjoying their tea, as they sipped delicately from beautiful rose-patterned china cups with gilt edges. Everybody looked so happy, so clean, and so rich. The portly, well-fed men looked out of the window at him with disdain as he peered through the glass, keen to have him shooed away. The head waiter marched towards Sheehan, and he fled. A fight was not going to impress Camilla.

Elijah's head was raging as he paced around the park, his head spinning about like a nervous guard on his first night's duty. When he saw her at a distance, she was strolling along a tree-lined avenue. With the afternoon sunlight shining down, in her white dress, she had the aura of an angel. Camilla had beautiful, ivory-coloured skin, brown hair, and soft eyes with long, lush lashes. She was deep in conversation with a debonair, well-dressed man as they walked along the path together.

Elijah made a few detours around the gardens, before finally planning to bump into her, 'by mistake'.

"Good afternoon, Mrs Iverson," he said, almost standing on her toes, he was so close. "You are Mrs Iverson, yes?"

The gentleman looked at him with contempt.

"I am so sorry, I do not know who you are?" she scolded, as she took a sidestep around him, keen to walk away.

He felt his temper rise again, throat and face reddening, jaw clenched, eyes wild with fury. He blocked her path. The man held Camilla's arm gently at the elbow.

"Is this gentleman bothering you, Camilla?" he asked in his upper-class nasal twang.

"No, Colin, it's fine. He was just on his way."

She gave Elijah a withering, condescending look. As she turned and walked away from him, he overheard her reassure the man:

"Oh, not to worry, Colin. He's somebody who worked for my husband—I think."

Elijah was filled with fury and hatred. He was belittled, ashamed and hopelessly outclassed. The bobby on patrol in the park watched him staring at the couple and made his way over to nip the nastiness in the bud.

"Come now, sonny. Move along, now. We don't want no trouble now, do we?"

"No, officer. She reminded me of my dear old ma, God rest her soul. That's why I was staring. I'll be off now," lied Elijah, not convincing the officer in the slightest.

Keeping a low-profile, he stalked Camilla and Colin at a distance for quite a while, staying out of sight while they sauntered along at a leisurely pace—a pace that only the well-off could afford. He hoped the man would walk

Camilla to her door. For once, luck was on Elijah's side. They strolled through one of the imposing wrought-iron gates and left the park. An evil smile replaced his deep frown.

The promenaders reached a magnificent white mews, lined with Palladian-looking buildings, their classical architecture obviously designed to reflect the character of the sophisticated people it housed. Camilla and her friend stopped at one of the front doors to exchange elaborate goodbyes. Then, the gentleman continued on his way and turned at the corner.

Elijah had stayed a reasonable distance away, ambling slowly. Camilla turned and began floating up the six steps from the cobbled street to the front door, looking for her key, which was proving elusive. He increased his pace and stealthily crept up behind. As she put her gloved hand on the doorknob, his grubby bare hand covered hers. It was getting towards twilight, and the mews was quiet. No one would rush over to help. The shame of shouting out and the neighbours discovering her at night with such a ruffian paralysed her momentarily. If he shouted out her name, they might correctly presume she knew the fellow, a thought she dreaded.

"Be a love. Open the door, Camilla," he whispered in her ear.

She could sense his hot, smelly breath, and the hairs rose on her neck and arms. Camilla twisted her head to look at him. His eyes were that of a desperate mad man.

His angular features contrasted by the strange evening light made him look like the devil himself. She was afraid and rightly so.

12

THE GLINT IN THE DARKNESS

A monstrous Sheehan pulled out a knife with a short blade and held it against her flawless cheek.

"No," she gasped.

"Am I too much of an Irish culchie for ye now?" he asked as the blade began to dig into her soft skin, threatening to slice it. "Now, Camilla, open the feckin' door and no shouting, eh, my lovely?"

She unlocked the hefty door, and let herself in, Elijah following closely behind, like an ominous shadow. To remind her that he had the knife to her ribs, he pricked her with its sharp point through her dress.

On opening the entrance, Elijah pushed Camilla roughly into the hallway. They made their way down the corridor to her flat's entrance. Once inside, she set about lighting the lamps. He cast a glance about him as the interior came into view, flame by flame. The reception room tiles were black and white marble and the walls were panelled in the lightest green damask silk.

Further inside, gilt-framed mirrors and elegant French furniture hugged the walls. Opening the double doors to the sitting room, it seemed as though golden sunshine emblazoned the room. Bright yellow chairs and floral settees enhanced the London orangey twilight flooding in. Elijah had never seen such a beautiful place, and probably never would again. Camilla stood behind the settee in an effort to distance herself from the odious intruder.

"So, this is how the rich live is it, Camilla?" He looked at her, venom in his eyes, and voice. "Just one of your husband's workers am I, eh?"

He gave a wry laugh. He helped himself to a large glass of liquor from the sideboard which he downed in one. Then he had another, filling the tumbler up to the brim this time. It befell the same swift demise as the first. Camilla looked at him, getting more irate with his rude and selfish behaviour.

"Imagine if I were to tell your lovely new neighbours the truth—you would be shunned. At least the lower classes are more forgiving."

"Why would they ever believe what an oik like you might say? Look at you, you common Irish rogue!" she sneered. "They would laugh at you."

She was deliberately humiliating him, and he felt it.

"Why did you ever take me to your bed, Camilla?"

"I must have been desperate," she laughed callously.

His pride might have been dented, and his fury escalating, but what he felt most was lust. Camilla's allure was still captivating. He made his way slowly around the floral settee.

"Be careful," he warned her, his finger under her nose. "You need to treat me with a bit more respect, else my tongue might wag loudly about the times we spent in bed together."

"Never, Elijah! Never! You will never fit into my world nor take it from me. You disgust me. And if you think you can blackmail me—you can think again!"

"Shut your trap," snarled Elijah, as he brandished the knife near her belly to show he was the one in control.

Rather than showing she was terrified, Camilla smirked. The desire to hurt her, bring her down a peg or two, silence that cruel tongue of hers was becoming overwhelming. Rage emanated from deep within Elijah's being.

Humiliated, he leapt at her, knocking her down with an iron fist to the head. Stunned, she fell onto her turquoise Oriental rug, hair framing her beautiful face. Now, standing over her as the drink turned up the intensity of his bravery, Elijah watched her squirm in her daze. He straddled her hips with his scrawny legs and put his left hand on her shoulder, pinning her down.

"Shush, now, me darlin'," he warned.

Petrified, Camilla did as she was told. Then before she could work out what would happen next, in a blur, Elijah raised the knife above his head, grabbing the handle so tightly his hand shuddered. Then, he plunged it down into her ribs, putting what little bodyweight he had fully behind it. He took great, silent pleasure in gliding the blade deep into her chest until she was dead.

He noticed blood started to seep into the posh rug. He stood up like a shot and smudged in the few splatters that had landed on his dark coat. Then he rubbed his face and hands to get them clean. Thankfully for Elijah, all the traces of blood on him could be hidden. He watched her, morbidly fascinated, as the stain got bigger and bigger. Then the reality of the moment caught up with him, and he panicked. The horror of the deed felt much worse than his fantasizing. He'd expected to find it easier, especially after all the brutal bludgeoning Sally suffered at his hand.

Determined to shake the shock off and get back to the task at hand, he marched across to the bedroom, a sliver of its pink and white rose-patterned curtains and bedspreads showing through the crack of the door. In the bay window was a blue-and-white Wedgewood urn full to bursting with sweet-smelling blooms. The elegant furniture was a delicate balance of style, and grace—but what it looked like wasn't what interested him—it was what it contained.

First, Elijah planned to rifle through all the drawers. He found a small antique music box that played a tune when the lid was opened. Inside, it was chock full of jewellery. He grinned as he stuffed it into his coat pocket. Putting a hand in the dressing-table drawer, he pulled out whatever he touched within. His light-fingered hand happened upon a gold locket with diamonds, and sapphires embedded in it. He wrapped it around his fingers. By the mirror was a shallow dish housing a sizeable engagement ring nestled amongst some others, plus some loose change. He helped himself to all that as well. He took the box out of his pocket and smiled as he added the latest finds. Then, he heard a noise—footsteps! His senses were on high alert. He froze briefly, then squeezed himself silently between two rosewood wardrobes in the bedroom hoping to conceal himself. There they were again. His heart was beating loudly in his chest as he held his breath in terror. Looking out towards the sitting room, he saw the lifeless body on the floor.

Moments later, with immense relief, he realised the sound was coming from the corridor outside the flat. Once the footsteps had faded, he stepped out of the recess. In his haste, he caught his coat sleeve on the ornate door edging. As he fought to free himself, he didn't notice one of his coat cuff buttons coming loose as he yanked. It rolled silently on the carpet, stopping at the skirting board. He struggled to put the antique box back in his coat.

Keen to flee the scene, he tiptoed into the sitting room and pinched one last essential item. On the sideboard was a silver tray of spirits. He grabbed the first bottle that came to hand, a full one of he knew not what, and put it into his long coat pocket. He glanced back at Camilla on the floor, and felt nauseous, beginning to regret things getting out of hand. He had only really meant to threaten her into giving him money. Nervously, he peered out of the doorway to her flat. Seeing a man exiting through the main door, he snapped his head back out of view. With his ear pressed hard to the door, so much so it was going numb, he listened out for more movements.

When the coast felt clear, he snuck out of the building. The air had cooled considerably as night fell. There was no wind. The sun had set behind the clouds, and the air was cool. The facades of the great houses surrounded by iron balustrades and gates seemed unreachable fortresses.

He was angry, envious, and covetous; he would never live in one of these houses. He walked through parks with their lakes clipped lawns, and topiary trees, everything designed to intrigue the already spoilt eye of the regular commuters.

Having put a big dent in the bottle of what turned out to be vodka, Camilla's demise was soon a distant memory. His ecstatic fingers played with the glittering haul of jewellery in his pocket. He had not felt this good in months. Even a five-shilling leg over wasn't this exciting. No one had seen him. He felt invincible.

The more he drank, the more cavalier his attitude became. He wanted to tell his underworld chums what he had done and how he had done it. *They will be in awe of my evil prowess. Those small-timers normally break windows or fingers to put the frighteners on people. I've gone up a league! I've rubbed someone out, just like that. I have to control myself. Keep schtum.* By the time the vodka had vanished, he was glad that he killed her. *Who did that hoity-toity harpy think she was, eh?*

Finally, he was back at the Blue Parrot. The return trip took longer—he lost an hour staggering and pausing to drink. Against his better judgement, he had not gone home to change his shirt or coat as planned, preferring, in his inebriated state to head directly to the pub.

His boozy bar buddies crowded around him, curious to know where he had been all day. He faced intense questioning but managed to lie convincingly. As more drink addled Elijah's brain, his earlier euphoria evaporated, his mood blackened. The more he drank, the nastier he became. By midnight he had started a fight with a man much bigger than he was, his trademark form of self-sabotage.

Towards the end of the brawl, Elijah could hardly speak, and his eyes were rolling around like marbles down a wooden chute. In that sorry condition, it only took one smack, and the cocky little chap was knocked out cold.

When Joe closed up, Elijah was still on the floor. There was no way on God's green earth that Joe was going to leave him in the bar all night. The last time Elijah feigned his drunkenness, he robbed a few bottles of grog to sell on the street before scarpering.

The frustrated barman dragged Elijah out onto the street by his feet, his head bouncing on every flagstone as he was unceremoniously ejected. Although Joe was enjoying giving Elijah his comeuppance, he stopped just short of the pub's double doors. A box had fallen out from under his coat. Joe knew it was stolen because it was far too beautiful, and expensive to belong to a nobody like Elijah Sheehan.

He put the jewellery box under the bar, without noticing that there was the name 'Camilla' engraved on it. Joe dragged the drunken Irishman the final two yards onto the cobbles, then locked up the pub. Going upstairs to his room, Joe grizzled about Elijah. He detested Sheehan with such vehemence that he genuinely believed that the man's death could only make the world a better place.

13

THE STRANGER RETURNS

The next day, early in the evening the customers were arriving in their droves at the Blue Parrot. It did not take Elijah long to find a mate to buy him a drink. His regular mates staggered in one by one, and each arrival bought a fresh round.

"Hey Elijah, ya know who I met the other day?"

"Who?"

"I swear it was ya wee lass, Ebba," said Jacky.

"Now, how would you know the looks of Ebba? I havena seen her for years. Not even me, her father, would recognise her now."

"I was in a bad way the other afternoon, and had no money on me, so I rented me a coffin. I shoulda bought me a bottle and slept on the street, but I felt so sick, I couldn't face a drink."

"And? What's this got to do with that girl o' mine?" asked Elijah, hoping the conversation would return to who was buying him a drink next.

"Well, I heard the boss lady calling, 'Ebba, Ebba!' I know yer lass was Ebba. Not too many of them in these parts now are there?"

"No. How old did she look?"

"About fourteen, I would say, and a right looker at that."

It was the best news that Elijah had heard for a long time. He had a daughter, he had contacts, and he was going to make a lot of money out of her if she was anything like her mother. *Especially if she's winsome.*

Elijah walked to the coffin house. The booze was beginning to wear off a little, and he was missing the buzz. He hadn't given thought to Ebba for years, but he was thinking about her a lot now. Fourteen was a very good age to introduce a girl to the real world. Sally was about that age when they met, and she ended up being a nice little earner.

He entered the coffin house by the front door. There was a queue ahead of him, and he pushed to the front. A man stopped him, took his arm, and guided him to the back of the line.

The name on his uniform said, 'Lieutenant Harrison.'

"I apologise sir, but we have an influx of people today. It takes a while to process them. Please be patient. We will get to you."

"I don't want a bed—I want to see the person in charge. That's why I walked to the front," demanded Elijah in the most assertive voice he could muster.

"Please stand aside, Sir. I will fetch Sergeant Major Chadwick," Harrison replied curtly, noticing the ill-mannered guttersnipe reeked of stale booze.

Elijah waited for what seemed like an age. He was struggling to maintain his temper. The revolting little man was shouting and abusing everybody around him when Jess arrived.

"And who are you then?" he asked rudely.

"Sergeant Major Chadwick," replied Jessica.

"I was expecting—a man," he said with disdain but still crassly staring at her chest.

"What is your business here? Are you a delivery man?" she asked him, ignoring the insult and his gawping expression. She felt his conduct so far summed up his probable character to a tee.

"You have my daughter, and I have come to fetch her," crowed Elijah.

"We don't keep unaccompanied children here. Perhaps you should try the orphanage or the workhouse?"

"My friends told me she was here, Missus, and friends don't lie, now do they?"

"What is her name?" asked Jessica, used to working with obnoxious drunks.

"Ebba" he replied," Ebba Sheehan."

Jessica was taken off guard, but she managed to keep her deadpan expression.

"Then you need to come in and speak to Colonel John Chadwick," she said professionally.

Jess and Elijah walked through rows and rows of coffin beds. He made lewd comments throughout the journey, and by the time they reached the steps to John's office, Jessica had made the decision that Ebba would not leave with this man—under any circumstances.

Jessica knocked on John's office door and waited.

"Come in!" was the shouty reply.

John looked up and saw Jessica accompanied by a small, bitter-looking man. His clothes were not too badly patched, but they were filthy with soot and gave off an atrocious smell. His hair and eyebrows were snowy white, and he had no teeth. He clearly led an unrelentingly harsh existence. For Colonel Chadwick, the most obvious thing about the reprehensible fellow's appearance—was his arrogance.

Ebba was sitting at her desk and turned around to see what was happening.

Despite what his gut was telling him, Colonel John Chadwick, ever the gentleman, shook Elijah's hand and introduced himself formally.

Without being offered a seat, Elijah sat down, crossed his skinny legs one over the other like a woman would, and began to speak with great authority.

> "Now, John, Colonel Chadwick, Sir, it has come
> to me attention, that you are keeping a wee lass
> here called Ebba Sheehan."

Ebba's eyes were fixed on the man. She recognised the voice, and the smell, even though she was on the other side of the room.

> "Go on," said John in a slow and measured tone.

Jessica was standing beside him, and she had already made the decision that Elijah would take the child away from her over her dead body. She hoped her husband concurred.

"Well, as we all know, the child is my property."

He paused, waiting for a response, but got none, so he decided to be more forthright.

"Now, I don't want to start any trouble, but I have come to fetch her, and take her home, as is my right," Elijah informed them arrogantly.

Ebba wanted to run out of the room—to escape. However, Jess glared at the girl with her customary look that implied Ebba needed to sit still in silence and woe betide her if she disobeyed. John had noted that in his semi-sober, argumentative state, Elijah had not even realised that there was a child in the room. *He's too busy throwing his weight around to see what is right under his nose.*

"Mr Sheehan, how old is your daughter?" asked John.

"Well, now let's see, she should be about fourteen or fifteen. Or perhaps thirteen."

"That doesn't sound very precise, Mr Sheehan. When last did you see the girl? You will have to provide us with a birth certificate before she can go with you, of course. You do understand?" explained John, being helpfully unhelpful.

Elijah felt his indignation begin to rise. He knew that neither he nor Sally had registered the child.

"Well, I last saw her when she was seven or eight. She was very bad, it looked like she suffocated her little brother in bed one night you know? Then she took to the streets. Aye, a child murderer, and one so young too. Well, it was probably an accident. But my son still ended up dead." He shook his head slowly. "I could not find her for years, and I searched, and searched. The grief, it eventually killed her poor mother."

Ebba could not keep quiet, it was lies, all lies. She felt anger well up in her, ashamed of the man that was her father, then she ran to Jessica's side. Elijah was surprised to see the girl appear from nowhere.

"Jess, John, you know this is all lies. I never killed my baby brother. I told you it was that man rolling on him when he was drunk. And as for grief killing my mother, well she was already dead by then!"

Jess pulled her close.

"Calm down, Ebba, I know you didn't harm little Kel, just stand here by me, you are safe with us."

She consoled the child who had rivers-worth of tears running down her face. Elijah looked at the girl closely.

Even with her red, puffed-up face, she is a beauty. Oh, how lucky I am. He stood up and walked around the desk.

> "Hello, my love! Oh, how I have missed you. My, but you are so grown up." He moved closer and closer to her. "I am yer Da' come to fetch ya, lass. We are all human. We all make mistakes. I have been so lonely without you."

He smiled his toothless smile, then took another step closer to his long-lost daughter.

> "You remember yer ol' Dad, do you not? Come now, Ebba, come give yer Da' a kiss hello."

He put out his filthy hand with its dirty nails to stroke her hair, but John Chadwick stood up and placed himself between Elijah and his daughter.

> "That's enough. Don't touch the girl. Jessica, I will deal with this matter. You and Ebba can go now."

Jessica didn't want to go anywhere. She wanted to stay behind, and hurt the little weasel. Ebba was traumatised. Still, both of them complied with her husband's wishes.

They ascended the iron stairs to the staff quarters, then went into the room Ebba shared with Suzanna. The beds were immaculately made. There were pictures on the wall that Ebba had made. The room was pale yellow, and Jessica wondered where they had salvaged the paint from. There was a pretty lacy cloth draped over a table. The room was cheerful and bright.

"Jess, I am not going with that man. I have never known him. I was raised by neighbours. I hate him, Jess. He is evil. All that smiling, and charm, but underneath he is the devil himself. I would rather be on the street than near him."

"Ebba, John and I will never let anything happen to you. The last thing we will allow is for that man to take you away. You are going to be a great woman one day, and the odious Mr Sheehan is not part of your future any more than he was part of your past."

Ebba began to calm down.

"Let's go by the back stairs, shall we? We can get some tea in the kitchen. That will make us feel much better."

Like two conspirators, they sneaked down the stairs to the scullery. All the while, Jessica was wondering what John was telling Elijah, but she daren't go back and leave Ebba alone.

Elijah was still in John's office. He had not anticipated such resistance from a religious man.

"So again, Elijah, what is your current job? And what is your address? You cannot take the girl to the streets or the pubs."

At the threat of curtailing his pub habit, Elijah almost lost his composure.

"Well you see, John, I have fallen on hard times, and well I thought that Ebba being family, she could get a small job, and with two incomes, we could support each other."

"Go on," said John, humouring him.

"Yea, that's how me and ol' Sally, Ebba's ma used to make ends meet. But you know, a thought just crossed my mind. If you want to keep the girl, how about you give me a wee something, and I will just be off, ye see that's all I need, just a wee something. A payment in lieu of her earnings isn't it, I suppose?"

"Elijah, Ebba is not going with you. We have rescued her from near death on the streets. Where were you then, man? I will tell you—you were in places like the Blue Parrot with your mates. I am giving you no money, for if I give to you once, you will always be back for more, and more, and more." explained John firmly.

"I have friends who can hurt you. Gawd, who do yer think yer are? I will go to the courts," shouted Sheehan.

"Now, please follow me," John replied calmly.

Elijah hurled abuse and expletives at John all the way to the front door where he handed Elijah to Lieutenant Harrison.

"Harrison, tell all your men that Elijah Sheehan may never come onto these premises ever again."

Harrison was an ex-army man, so he was well equipped to deal with rabble-rousers.

"And from now on, Harrison, you will escort Ebba to, and from school every day.

"Yes, Sir!" replied Harrison, secretly wishing that he could give the man a good clobbering. *Perhaps he might have a mishap down a dark alley one night?*

Jess and Ebba were back in John's office.

"Right, now the two of you, listen up. No more larking about on the streets on your way home from school, Ebba. Harrison will accompany you everywhere you go. He will keep you safe."

"Yes, John," answered Ebba

He felt sorry for the child, not only for the trauma of the evening, per se, but also having a father like the repugnant Elijah Sheehan. He would not discuss that with her for fear of adding to the horrid thoughts she was probably dealing with already.

That evening before retiring to bed, John and Jessica spoke about the situation.

> "Jessica, we need to speak to Mrs McAlistair. I am afraid that if Ebba remains here, Elijah will eventually get to her. We will still see her. I know you adore the child, but we must think of her future."

> "John, this is so difficult for me. We have had her from a wee little thing. She has been through so much. I cannot believe that a loving father would leave it all these years to look for his daughter. He did not even know what she looked like and was vague about her age."

John sighed.

> "Jess, there are some people that we can never reform. That is not a Godly opinion, of course, but we have worked with these people for years now, and there are some men who are pure evil. From what I saw today, Elijah Sheehan is one of them."

Jessica fell asleep, but she slept fitfully and had nightmares about the devious and deceitful father.

Despite Ebba's emotional turmoil, she went to school the next day and took her exam. She had scored well in all her subjects, but this was the most important one because mathematics did not come naturally to her, it needed work.

People always said that only boys could do mathematics. Still, John said that was nonsense, and that Ebba would beat Gerry Taylor hands down in the exam if she practised enough.

Ebba scored an A grade. Nobody was as proud as John because he had been helping her, providing some extra private tuition. Bunty made a cake, and they all celebrated together around the scullery table. Ebba seemed to have got over her fright of seeing Elijah Sheehan, and Harrison was ever vigilant.

Eventually, the only people left at the table were John, Jess and Ebba.

"Ebba, I have a question," said John.

She looked at him and nodded for him to proceed.

"Why do you want to be a nurse?" he asked.

"I want to help people, John, I've already told you that. Please don't try and change my mind."

John smiled. The child had spirit.

"Why not be a doctor?" he enquired, as Jess studied the girl's expression.

She looked at him for a long time.

"I never thought I could get that far," she replied. "It's easy for girls like me from poor backgrounds to become nurses, but a doctor, I don't know. Can't only men be doctors?"

"Well, my girl, Gerry Taylor thought only boys could do mathematics, and we showed him that wasn't true."

"The thing is, Ebba," advised Jess," for the next part of your education, there will need to be changes. You will need to live in the heart of the city with Mrs McAlistair, and go to the university in London."

Ebba looked distressed.

"I don't want to leave here."

"You won't leave us. Look at Elliot. He is studying to be a doctor, and he comes to visit."

"Does Elliot also stay at Mrs McAlistair's?" asked Ebba innocently.

"No lass, Elliot is off doing some studying overseas. He's got quite a flair for medicine."

"And Elijah. Will he be able to find me?"

"Never," said John," Elijah will never bother you again, lass, and if he does, we will go to the police."

"Who will pay for me to study?" asked Ebba, concerned about her impoverished background.

"The Salvation Army has a medical corps, and there are scholarships for very clever people, like you, to become doctors, and work for the organisation." John explained.

It was a lot to absorb. Ebba was too excited to sleep, and kept Suzanna awake till well past midnight, jabbering on about the new plan. Eventually, Suzanna told her to be quiet, but Ebba got no sleep, and she yawned in all of her classes the next day.

14

ANOTHER NIGHT IN THE COLD ALLEYWAY

It was opening time at the Blue Parrot. After a rough night sleeping in a doorway, Elijah was awakened by the cold. It was a miracle he had survived the night. Through the window, he saw Joe behind the bar counter, polishing the glasses for the lunchtime rush.

He opened the bar doors and got the welcoming whiff of stale beer from the night before. Now, Joe was washing off the tables and benches. He'd been away for a few days to tend to his ailing mother and wasn't delighted to be back.

"Johnny could have at least let me sleep in here last night. It might be spring, but it's brass monkeys out there! I woke up with frost on me!" said Elijah with a sour attitude.

"You will never freeze," replied Joe," too much alcohol running through your veins."

Still not liking Elijah at all, Joe smirked at his overnight hardship. Having watched how Sheehan had treated Sally, he thought he was a slippery snake. On several occasions, he had tried to intervene, but they were like two peas in a pod, both as bad as each other, and he gave up. He thought back to the night Sally died of exposure after collapsing in the alleyway. It weighed on his conscience. Joe knew that Elijah had at least one child with Sally, and rumours abounded about how he treated their daughter in her early years. However, he had never seen the girl and Elijah never spoke of her. He prayed that wherever she was that she was safe—if she was still alive, unlike her poor little brother and mother.

"By the way, there's something of yours under the bar. You left it when you were sozzled, and I had to drag you out a few days ago."

A curious Elijah fumbled around the deep shelf under the countertop, wondering what other treasures he could pocket from the lost property. He saw the antique casket amongst all the glasses and empty wallets on the far left of the shelf. He stood bent over for a minute or so perusing what else might take his fancy until Joe snapped at him:

"That's it. The box. Now take it, and get your sticky mitts out of there!"

He put the beautiful box on the old wooden bar top, fiddling with the awkward clasp at eye level. Once undone, he threw the lid back. A feeble, tinkling tune began to play. It sounded eerie, and out of place in the gritty East End pub, more used to a drunken pianist bashing out a loud tune on the ivories. He snapped the mechanism off to silence it. He grinned as he toyed with the jewellery. He wasn't sure why Joe thought it was his, but he was happy to take it off his hands.

It looked worth a few bob, and Elijah was keen to shift it. He snapped it shut and quickly shoved it in his pocket. He skipped out of the pub straight onto the road.

The streets were busy even though the day was miserable, grey, and dark. The market place looked like a black and white photograph. Nobody wore anything of colour. It was raining. Soot and grime were running off the roofs and down the sides of the building, causing the red brick to become a deathly black.

He turned left into Lark Street. It was more like an alleyway than a road. It would be difficult to get a carriage through it. He walked to number nineteen, a shabby two-up-two down. The front door was chipped, and the nine of the number was hanging upside down like a six.

It was opened by a sinewy, oldish-looking man with yellowish greying hair, two days of stubble on his chin, and a fag hanging from his mouth. You would never have guessed him to be forty-five. Alcohol had ravaged his liver, and it was obvious that he would not live to see old bones.

"Eli, my old mucker! What brings you here so early then?" asked Jimmy.

"Jimmy, I have something I need to shift. Take a look at it, will yer?"

"How many more times! Not on the street, come inside."

The house was surprisingly clean except for nicotine stains on the walls. A tiny gaunt woman greeted Elijah and then disappeared upstairs. She knew the routine well. If strangers arrived, she went away until they left. It was all a part of Jimmy's business, and he never wanted her involved. Sheehan could never work out if she was Jimmy's wife or not.

Elijah removed the jewellery box from under his coat. He tried to hand it over but failed. Jimmy had clocked the name faintly engraved on the top of the box which read: 'Camilla'.

"Oh no lad, I'm not touching that."

"What do you mean, Jimmy? I always bring you good stuff, and this is probably worth a few hundred quid."

"No, Elijah, it's worth nothing."

"Why are you saying that? What's got into you? What about the jewellery inside, you haven't even seen that!" snarled a disappointed Elijah.

"Get out of me house, Sheehan. You obviously haven't read the newspaper this morning. Take the box with you, and don't come by again."

"But we have been doing business for years Jimmy, why now?"

Elijah thought if he demonstrated the jewellery he might have more luck. As he looked down, preparing to battle with the clasp again, he saw the word 'Camilla.' The memory hit him like a train.

"Get out of me house you stupid murdering swine."

He left Jimmy's, barely able to breathe because of the shock. He slid the jewellery box back into his big inside coat pocket. His thumb poked through a hole in the lining that he had not noticed before. Feeling down towards the hem, he found his blade knife. He tore at the stitching and retrieved it. There was blood encrusted on the handle and even more on the blade.

He was in trouble. He hid it in his other inside pocket. Fortuitously, a shilling rolled out of the hole he made in the hem of his coat. He picked it up and clutched it in his hand, tightly, then headed off to the nearest pub.

"Whiskey. Irish. And make it a double," he ordered.

He quaffed the drink in one, hoping it would numb his nerves, but it barely touched the sides of his deep anxiety. The antique box was well hidden under his coat, but he had no idea what to do with it. He was too afraid to keep it with him. Equally, he was too scared to let it go because it was very valuable, and would solve a lot of his money worries if he could shift it on.

Elijah was stunned. How could Jimmy have known what happened in the flat? Sure, he saw Camilla's name, but what was his talk about the newspaper, and worse— murder.

Elijah retraced his steps, back down Lark Street and then to the market square. He felt as if everybody was watching him. He made his way to a newspaper stand and heard the paperboy shouting:

"Camilla Iverson murdered! Clifford Iverson's wife murdered."

Elijah would have preferred another drink with the last of his money but had to buy a newspaper instead. The article read thus:

MILLIONAIRE'S WIFE MURDERED

The wife of Clifford Iverson, millionaire shipbuilder, was found yesterday in her Mayfair flat murdered. She had not been seen for a few days and officers had to break down the door to investigate her unexplained disappearance.

Camilla Iverson (née FitzAlan) was killed by force, and police believe that she may have interrupted a robbery as some items of value were taken.

If anybody can assist with the investigation, please contact Chief Inspector Mason at the Mayfair and Soho Constabulary.

Elijah went into a tailspin, knowing he would have to gather himself, or he was going to hang. He thought back to the day in question. *What if the man she was walking with remembers me? The police might talk to him? There is nothing I can do—except hide this bloody box somewhere til the dust settles. Only two people know about the box so far: Joe the barman, and Jimmy the fence, but can I trust them to shut up? Joe never discusses anyone's business, but is a wild card—and hates me. I bet he would love to see me meet my maker. Buying stolen goods is Jimmy's business, so he'll have a natural reluctance to say anything to the coppers. So, he's less of a problem, but he'll save his skin before mine.*

Elijah didn't like the look of how this was panning out at all.

15

TELL ME ABOUT YOUR WIFE

Clifford Iverson sat in Chief Inspector Mason's office. The small room looked neat and official. There were shelves with law books upon them, a large desk covered in papers and some grainy black and white portrait photographs in simple wooden frames. The shipyard magnate presumed they were Mason's family. The officer was dressed in an average-priced grey tweed suit.

He began by thanking Clifford for coming to see him, then cut straight to establishing some facts.

"Sir, you, and your wife, Camilla Iverson, were separated, is this true?"

"Yes, Sir. Divorced, actually," replied Clifford.

"I see," said Mason as he scratched some notes down with his fountain pen. "May I enquire as to why?"

"Some years ago, she had a passionate affair with another man. I caught them in bed together at the family home. I was devastated, furious, humiliated by Camilla—but I could never harm her," replied Clifford, earnestly. "In fact, I helped her set up her new life in Mayfair, in that wretched flat—where—where you found her."

At that, Mason scribbled down a lot more notes, then looked up over his half-moon glasses.

"And when did you last see her?"

"The day I met her in Mayfair and gave her the keys to a new, bigger flat she was moving to. She needed more space for when our sons visited. They're adolescents now, and they shot up in the last year or so. I still wanted their mother to be part of their lives, if not mine. Now, let me think—that would be about seven weeks ago now. I can check the exact date with the estate agent," replied Clifford.

"Were you angry with her? Maybe the old wound of betrayal flared up again in your mind? Or perhaps having to pay more towards her upkeep for all those years? It can't be easy with the expense of running two households and no wife to oversee the running of your own home."

"Of course, I was angry with her!" barked Clifford his voice rising. "The love of my life humiliated me. My sons would have been the laughing stock of their school if word got out, so I divorced her quietly. I paid off the newspaper owners handsomely to not report it. There were rumours of course, loose talk amongst the workers, but with the press silenced, not much proof. The deal was I bought her a flat, and told her she was never to contact me again."

"How did she respond to that?" asked the Chief Inspector.

"It was like she realised she had killed the goose that laid the golden egg. She begged me for forgiveness, but I couldn't forgive. I had done all I could to give her the best life possible. She had everything—everything." Clifford wanted to cry, but he could not lose his composure in front of this officer.

"Sir, I know this is difficult, but many partners in higher social circles commit adultery, and life goes on. If I may be so vulgar, tongues have wagged, and the press has had a field day about Princess Louise being unfaithful to the Duke of Argyll with a string of men. And yet, they are still husband and wife. Why could you not follow suit?"

"For two reasons, Sir," replied Clifford. "I am not like people of the high social ranks. I am more of a self-made man. Further, the lothario she had an affair with was a petty criminal and drunkard who was married to a prostitute. His mouth ran away with him in many an East End pub, and he ensured every man at the shipyard, or neighbouring docks knew that he had—fornicated—with my wife. That was how I found out. My accountant came to me with the sorry news. I didn't believe him at first, and the affair continued. I was an object of intense ridicule at the dockyards and my workshops.

"Who was this petty criminal?"

"A man called Elijah Sheehan. I first saw him when I disturbed them at my stables. He ran out like a naked greyhound clutching his clothes. Obviously, we didn't speak." said Clifford, simmering with rage and sadness.

Chief Inspector Mason was quiet. The man who sat before him was highly emotional. His years of experience with the force gave him a feeling in his gut that the man was telling him the truth, something which was a breath of fresh air in his occupation.

"Did you ever confront him, later I mean, Mr Iverson?"

"No."

"Why not?" asked the inspector.

"Because he would have enjoyed seeing my pain. He looked the cruel sort that would revel in my despair."

"Did you ever see him again?"

"Yes. I spoke to my manservant and asked him to get me some ragged clothes as a disguise. My accountant told me which pubs my men tended to frequent, and I did a tour of all of them. I found him in the Blue Parrot one night. He seemed to have great charisma because everybody tried very hard to get his attention."

"Where did they meet each other."

For the first time throughout the interview, Clifford could not speak. Eventually, he dropped his head into his hands.

"In my home," he answered. "We wanted to have the garden landscaped. Sheehan lied saying he was an experienced groundsman and had worked for many industrialists in the area. He offered to do some plans for the garden. I was away, but since it was an urgent requirement, my wife invited him inside to discuss them. She said he looked quite well to do when she first met him. He had a smart coat and decent shoes. Quite business-like, she said. That was the first time I knew of him, but back then, I didn't know he was offering—additional services. When I saw him in the pub, the night I followed him a few months later, he looked more like an oversized chimney sweep."

"Just to be clear, did you want to kill your wife when you found out?" asked the inspector.

"Of course I wanted retribution, but I did not murder Camilla. I don't want to make work for the hangman, do I?"

"Did you know if they continued the affair after you discovered Sheehan at the stables?"

"I honestly don't know. I lost all trust in our relationship. I cut myself off from her, except financially. I think that I was more than fair. I expect she terminated the affair shortly after. I suspect it was all a ploy to be free of me. It was not a physical craving, romance or love. Camilla liked to put on a show of how wealthy she was, be one of the social elite, not a mere housewife. Being seen with a vagabond like Sheehan would have put a hole below the waterline to that dream." He sighed. "I have four sons, and their mother may have been a bitter disappointment to them, but I was not going to let them down. I wanted to make sure I limited their suffering as much as possible."

"What are their ages," Chief Inspector Mason enquired.

"Nine, twelve, fifteen, and seventeen," answered Clifford.

"Those poor lads. I am sorry, Sir,"

"So am I," said Iverson.

Mason stood up to show that the interview was over. The men shook hands before the officer showed Iverson out of his office.

What a nice gentleman, Mason thought. *But remember even nice gentlemen are known to murder their wives out of jealousy.*

Elijah did not know how he was going to survive the next few days. Most of the stolen goods he fenced were through Jimmy. For years, they had a good thing going between them. Suddenly, it felt as though the whole criminal underworld was shunning him. He would have to travel to Birmingham. They had a fine jewellery quarter, and perhaps he could fence his cursed haul there—or at least get it melted down and made into something else.

Another option was Manchester, there was a lot of money there. The last try would be Edinburgh, but travelling there cost a lot of money. The box and jewels could set him up for a long time—if only somebody wanted to take them.

Then he had a brainwave. He knew what he would do— he would sit polishing the case until he abrased the name off.

Elijah was confused, angry and desperate for a drink. After plodding along in a trance, deep in thought, somehow he ended up at the Blue Parrot, hoping to cadge a few shots of whiskey off the lads. He wouldn't be going back for a while.

Across town, Chief Inspector Mason let himself into Camilla's flat.

16

VISITING MAYFAIR

Large and impressive, the flat was immaculately clean. It was only the portion of bloodied carpet that put a dampener on the exquisite décor and stunning views.

For a man wronged, Clifford Iverson had certainly provided his wife with a more than adequate lifestyle after her adulterous philandering.

He walked through the entire flat. There was the sitting room where the body was found. There were no bloody footprints anywhere. The rug had absorbed everything, apart from a patch that had soaked into the floor. Other than that, the bleeding had been quite localised. No arterial wounds. He made a note of how he had found the rug, then rolled it up as evidence for the court case. He made a plan to swap it with one of the large rugs from another room, keen to spare poor Mr Iverson any more hardship, if and when he returned to the property.

The shock of seeing the bloodstain would not be good for his already weakened constitution.

Chief Inspector Mason scoured each room in the flat. It seemed that the four sons slept two boys to a room when they visited. There was a guest room and Camilla's master bedroom. The dining room and Camilla's also had balconies but faced a beautiful square surrounded by black, iron railings. The inspector got to Camilla's bedroom, thinking that even on the worst winter day she would have woken up in paradise. The pink-and-white theme created a very light, airy feminine tone.

Slowly and methodically, Mason began to go through each drawer. Then he planned to move onto the cupboards. The murderer was clearly disturbed because the entire bureau was filled with priceless treasures, but he, or she, didn't have time to take everything. The first and only things that were seen were grabbed; namely, the jewellery box and whatever was placed in the shallow ceramic dish. That suggested to the officer that the burglar was not familiar with her routine. It was somebody who had never been there before. He looked under the bed, under all the furniture, and then he began to look through the large rosewood wardrobes that were so big that they almost stretched to the ceiling. There was just enough space for a child or small adult to hide in the gap between them.

He laughed, sure that one of her younger boys would have squeezed in there at some stage in a game of hide and seek. His eyes travelled to the floor, and something twinkled for a split second. He stood in every position he could, but he couldn't make the light reflect on the item again, it was a complete fluke that he had seen it. He got on his hands, and knees, and felt for it, but his arms were too short, and could not reach far enough. He walked to a utility cupboard near the entrance and fetched a broom. Pushing the brush towards the back of the space, it took five attempts to jam the bristles in at different angles to try to recover the item. Each time he brought the head to the front, he had retrieved nothing. On the final attempt, when he was beginning to think he had perhaps been seeing things, he bent over and picked up a button that belonged on the cuff of a coat. A small one that might be part of a decorative group of four or five. It was brass with a shamrock embossed upon it. *Well, well, well!*

Chief Inspector Mason put the button into his pocket for safekeeping, then went back to his small office, where he furiously scribbled down everything pertaining to the case. He rested his pen on the desk then boomed:

"Smith!"

"Yessir!" said the young constable almost instantaneously, keen to avoid an ear-bashing for tardiness from his superior.

"Yes. Please come here a moment," said Chief Inspector Mason to his assistant.

The young man marched into the room, his uniform immaculate. Mason could tell he was proud of his job.

"I have a challenge for you. I found a button at the Iverson flat this afternoon. It was under a wardrobe in the deceased's bedroom. I need you to find out who makes them," requested the Chief Inspector. "This may give us a clue as to who stabbed Camilla Iverson to death. It might belong to a removals chap since she had not long moved in there, but my copper's nose tells me it has something to do with her murder."

The young constable rolled the button around his fingertips as he inspected it.

"I know I can count on you to come up with something," Mason said encouragingly.

"Oh, one thing, Guv. What was the name of the man Mrs Iverson had an affair with?" asked the constable.

"Elijah Sheehan."

17

YOU'LL TAKE THE SERVANT'S STAIRS

Mrs McAlistair's house was like nothing that Ebba had experienced before. She had never seen so many refined objects in her life.

"Welcome, young lady," Mrs McAlistair greeted the girl.

"Good day, Ma'am," replied Ebba, wondering if she should curtsy.

The entrance hall of the four-storey house was the size of a small barn. A massive crystal chandelier hung from the ceiling high above the square stairwell down to the reception area. She guessed it must have been at least thirty feet long since it ended ten feet from the ground. The floors were white marble, and the walls were lined with floral silk fabric in rich red, and green. All the mouldings were painted gold, and Ebba couldn't convince herself that Buckingham Palace could be grander than this.

"Molly," called Mrs McAlistair, as she rang a little silver bell.

A young servant girl appeared. She was only a few years older than Ebba. They greeted each other with a smile.

"Molly will show you to your room. It is not a large space, after all, it is a favour to Colonel Chadwick, but we have found somewhere where we can squeeze you in."

"Thank you, Mrs McAlistair."

"There are a few house rules. You may only socialise with the family when you are invited to. You will eat in the kitchen with the servants. Finally, you are not allowed any visitors."

"Yes, thank you, Ma'am."

"Molly, take Ebba up to her room, and get her comfortable."

Ebba made for the huge staircase.

"Excuse me, my dear," said Mrs McAlistair, only the family is to use that staircase. Molly will show you the servants' steps.

"My apologies, Ma'am. Yes, of course, thank you."

Molly took her to the kitchen entrance and introduced her to the staff. They did not seem very friendly, in fact, Ebba felt they were a downright miserable bunch. Mrs Shaw, the housekeeper, was a tall, disconsolate-looking woman, who looked down her nose when she spoke to anybody. The butler, Mr Carrington was aloof, and there was no humour in his countenance.

There was not enough time to be introduced to anybody else as she was rushed through the scullery and off to the servant's stairs. Ebba glanced at the room. It was filled with all the mod-cons. It had a marble floor and large bay windows that flooded the room with light. There were two large black stoves and an icebox. She had never seen an icebox before.

There were cupboards from floor to ceiling, holding crockery of all different designs, and colours. Molly told her that all the silver was locked away, and only Mr Carrington and Mrs Shaw had the keys to those cupboards.

"Don't worry about anything, Ebba," said Molly kindly. "My room is next to yours, so we can look after each other. Oh, by the way, we share a bathroom."

Ebba began to relax. Molly seemed a lot more likeable than the others in the house, and she was grateful the girl would be close by.

They climbed to the top floor. Molly led her to a door, then opened it. The area was virtually the size of a cupboard. There was a tall, narrow set of drawers for her clothes, a desk with a lamp upon it, and a bed with pillows, blankets, and eiderdowns. There was a window in the roof that allowed in light. That was a blessing.

"You are lucky, Ebba," Molly confessed. "You can come and go as you wish to attend your lessons. I am stuck here all the time. I only get one Sunday off every second week."

Ebba hadn't been exposed to the life of the rich, and she had no idea how cruel, and rigorous a servant's life was.

"I've got to go now, Ebba. We can chat tonight when I'm off duty. If you need anything, just shout."

After a rather bland evening meal, eaten in silence, Ebba decided to retire to her room and get plenty of rest for her first day of proper study.

The London School of Medicine for Woman was imposing. Ebba was only fifteen, and too young to formally attend, and there were several subjects that she had to qualify in to be accepted for her medical degree. She spent a lot of time visiting various tutors.

It might have been tough, but it was fun. What a great adventure it was to see the sights of bustling London, the largest city in the world. She was comfortable in her little room at Mrs McAlistair's. On the Sundays when Molly had a day off, they would go out together and stroll through the parks sometimes stopping to have tea and cake as a treat. John and Jessica Chadwick gave her a modest stipend to sustain herself, with the agreement that she would pay back her scholarship by serving time working for the Salvation Army wherever they may need her.

After a particularly long day, her biology class, she returned to the scullery, exhausted. Her tutor Mr Williams was a real curmudgeon. Feeling drained, all she wanted was a slice of bread and a cup of tea.

"Hey, Ebba!" called Molly as she stood by the deep sink.

"Molly, how has your day been. I am shattered."

"Mrs Shaw wants to see you as soon as possible."

"Oh, my word, what have I done?"

"Not sure," laughed Molly," but you don't work for her, so I'm sure you won't be in trouble."

Ebba had a knot in her stomach whenever she approached Mrs Shaw, the woman was so professional, and she had never seen her smile or make any casual remarks.

"Are you looking for me, Mrs Shaw?" asked Ebba politely.

"Yes, Mrs McAlistair has invited you to dinner tomorrow evening at eight o'clock. The dress code is formal."

"I don't have a formal dress!" shrieked Ebba, panicking.

"That won't do. I will tell Molly to find you something."

She called Molly over to her.

"Take Ebba to the storeroom where they keep all the clothes that are donated to the Salvation Army. Find her a smart dress, good enough to wear to dinner tomorrow night, please?"

"Yes Ma'am," answered Molly, winking secretly at Ebba.

The service corridors wove inside the house like a maze, and she was sure she would never find her way back to the kitchen without Molly. Finally, they arrived in the storeroom.

"What is this place?" asked Ebba.

"Well, some wealthy people give their old clothes to charity. Or sometimes it's when a family member dies, and there is no one to hand it down to. Mrs McAlistair stores them up here until they are collected to be distributed or sold, depending on the quality of them."

It took two hours for the girls to decide on the correct outfit for Ebba. Molly could be in a lot of trouble when she got back to the kitchen, but she was under the instruction of Mrs Shaw, so she hoped nobody would reprimand her. Ebba and Molly had the greatest fun trying on garments of all shapes, and sizes. But it was the hats that had them in fits of laughter. *How could people think that putting these giant plumed things on their heads looked stylish?* Finally, they found Ebba a peacock blue silk dress with a lace collar. It was smart and not too sophisticated. They thought she would feel at ease; dressed up rather than trussed up in it.

"Leave your hair down for a change, Ebba. Do you have a necklace to wear with it?"

Ebba burst into fits of giggles.

"Of course not! What a question, Molly!"

The next evening, Ebba descended the steps into the kitchen feeling like royalty in the blue. She looked beautiful. Her hair hung down her back, and the colour of the dress suited her eyes and colouring.

Everybody turned to look at her. She was charming. But when Mrs Shaw saw the girl, her jaw dropped.

"Oh, bugger!" she yelled.

The whole kitchen staff turned to look at the woman who never put a professional foot out of place.

"Mr Carrington, we have an emergency, please come here," she ordered. This was not the correct order of command, so the butler was aghast.

By now, the whole kitchen was crowded about the beautiful Ebba, wondering what the rumpus was about.

"Mr Carrington, do you recognise this dress?" demanded Mrs Shaw.

"No, Ma'am, I do not."

"Anyone in this room recognise this dress?" bellowed Mrs Shaw.

"I don't," mumbled a worried Molly, responsible for choosing it.

"Oh, yes, Mrs Shaw," came an answer from the washroom. "That dress belonged to Master Arthur's fiancé, Miss Betty. She wore it to dinner last Christmas," explained Madge.

"I thought so! Oh, bloody hell, she will be here tonight! We can't allow this child to be embarrassed. We have one hour to find another dress. Madge come with us. You know which clothes belonged to whom. Molly, hurry up and get Ebba undressed. I will meet you in the storeroom in five minutes. Go to your room, Ebba. Now!"

Nobody had ever seen Mrs Shaw speak or behave this way. It was as though a ship was sinking, and she was taking control of a lifeboat. The four women tore up the stairs, with Ebba very confused.

Madge, the washerwoman, was in the storeroom rummaging through the clothes, flinging them in all directions until she pulled out a pale pink gown with a mother-of-pearl, bead-encrusted trim.

"They will never remember this one." said Madge "because it was never worn in this country. It belonged to some major's wife who died in Greece. Apparently, she had never worn it. Let's not let Ebba know of its provenance, ladies."

They scuttled back to Ebba's room, smoothing out the fabric, hoping it would look presentable. They slipped it over Ebba's head. She looked radiant, and the pale colour on the young girl created an air of innocence. They brushed her hair, pinched her cheeks, and all raced back to the kitchen. This time the staff were speechless. Ebba was a vision of beauty.

"Anybody recognise this dress?" demanded Mrs Shaw, with her usual brusque matronly tone used in a crisis.

"No, Ma'am!" came the united response.

"Good! Now, come here, Ebba. Turn around."

Ebba found herself twirled around by the shoulders as Mrs Shaw manoeuvred the girl into position like a whirlwind before she could even respond. Mrs Shaw reached into her apron pocket and drew out a delicate locket that twinkled in the light. Everybody watched, mesmerised, as the head housekeeper put the necklace on Ebba, a fine chain accompanying a tiny silver heart.

"It's been loaned by Mrs Chadwick. Look after it, now."

Ebba looked down and felt the cold, smooth metal with the delicate fingertips of her right hand. She thought the necklace was even more exquisite than the dress she found herself stood in. She looked at her reflection in the window pane, blackened by the dark night outside. Thinking back to being in rags in the alcove, huddled over the hot-air grate, she was stunned by her own image. *I don't recognise myself.* Her reverie was broken by the shrill tone of Mrs Shaw's voice penetrating the excited atmosphere in the kitchen.

"Come on! Come on! Shake a leg, girl! It is five to eight," she ordered. "Mr Carrington, please show Ebba the way to the dining room."

Ebba had no time to say thank you. Mr Carrington took the youngster by the arm and guided her upstairs.

"Nobody in this house is going to make a fool of that girl on my watch," announced Mrs Shaw, as she smoothed down her apron and checked not a hair was out of place.

The whole kitchen applauded.

"Get on with your jobs, now, please! We have a busy night ahead of us."

With that, Mrs Shaw was back to business.

Mr Carrington opened the door for Ebba and whispered in her ear:

"I seated you next to Elliot Chadwick so that you feel comfortable. Just watch which knives, and forks the others use for each course, and open your napkin on your lap. Oh, and Ebba, one more thing—you look lovely tonight."

Ebba had no time to ask Carrington about Elliot because when she turned around, the butler was gone. She was still dazed by the comedic uproar that had preceded her arrival at dinner.

Jess and Suzanna had taught her the fundamentals of table etiquette, but she had never practised it. She desperately tried to make sure the voice that was loudest in her head was the one telling her how she was supposed to conduct herself.

Having not seen Elliot for a long time, she tried to reckon how old he might be these days. She guessed about twenty-one, which seemed so grown up compared to her. He was a man now and as good as it was to be seated next to somebody familiar, she felt somewhat intimidated. He probably wasn't anything like the young lad who had saved her life from the snow that night anymore. These days, he was a man of the world, studying in America. Soon, he would be a fully qualified doctor.

Mrs McAlistair introduced Ebba to her family.

"Good evening, Ebba," greeted George McAlistair, with a friendly face. "I am so pleased to meet you. It is an honour to have another doctor living under our roof."

"Not yet a doctor, Sir, but someday," answered a modest Ebba with a broad, beautiful smile.

"Yes," continued George, "Elizabeth Barrett, and Elizabeth Blackwell have had a great influence on young women who want to practise medicine. Of course, you will be attending the university that she helped found."

"Yes, Sir. That is correct."

"Aren't you afraid of entering a man's world, my dear?" He asked sweetly.

"Sir, my mentor Colonel Chadwick says that I can do anything a man can do."

Ebba heard a chuckle behind her.

"That sounds just like my father."

She turned around to see Elliot standing there, dark, handsome, and so refined.

"Hello, Ebba," he smiled.

"Elliot, I am so glad to see you. I was terrified of not knowing anybody tonight." She blurted out in a whispered tone.

"You look beautiful," he confessed.

"If you knew the palaver that went with finding this dress and transforming me into 'a lady' you would have a good laugh. One day I'll tell you about it."

Elliot looked at Ebba. *She is lovely. That long, wavy hair to her waist, those bright eyes, and the most radiant smile. That starving, half-frozen little bundle I carried into the coffin house that night has become a lovely young lady.*

Two very handsome young men introduced themselves to Ebba. They were Mrs McAlistair's sons, Richard and Arthur. Both sons worked in their father's law firm. Richard was twenty-three, a dark-haired, good-looking man. He seemed to have a reserved tone about him, not serious, but respectful. Arthur was a year or two older and quite different in temperament. Ebba decided it was obvious he was a cad. He was overly charming and smooth.

Betty Carmichael, Arthur's fiancée, was of an unforgiving class, brittle, and spiteful.

Betty shook Ebba's hand without meeting her gaze.

"Oh, you do look lovely, my dear," she remarked loudly. "Where did you get your dress from it is rather unusual for a British designer?"

"Thank you very much, Betty. It was made in Greece," replied Ebba.

Betty gave her a condescending look, not quite masked with a fake smile, then drifted off into the corner to speak to Arthur.

"Was it really made in Greece?" whispered Elliot in her ear.

"Yes, just not for me!" she laughed.

18

THE NEEDLE IN THE HAYSTACK

Constable Smith was relentless in his search for the company that made the button with the shamrock embossed upon it. He walked from tailor to tailor in Savile Row. Eventually, he found an elderly man who showed some interest, Mr Davies.

"Let me take a look at that, constable," directed the old man.

The little tailoring shop was but a square in the wall with bolts of fabric stacked to the roof, a cutting table, and a sewing machine. Constable Smith carefully dropped it in the tailor's cupped palm. The old man pushed his glasses up the bridge of his nose, then peered at the button, pushing it about with his finger.

"Ah. Yes. Well, I am sure I don't need to tell you that it was made by an Irish tailor. But you might not know that this is very old. The faint tarnishing on this post at the back of the button tells me the garment was—I suspect— purchased a long time ago. There seems to be something etched onto it. Let me get my magnifying glass."

Constable Smith watched Mr Davies rifling through several drawers, praying he didn't drop the button accidentally, and it roll away somewhere awkward in the little shop. It was stuffed to the gills with stock and finding it again would be hellish.

Finally, he located the magnifying glass, and he gently kneed the drawer shut.

Davies turned the button around, inspecting the magnified item with great care. A suspenseful Smith looked on, wishing the old man would speed up and tell him something useful.

"Ah, now look at this lad, see this here—" Davies said jabbing at the button and giving Constable Smith a beckoning look to come and examine what was about to be revealed.

"—there is fine writing on the back. With the naked eye, it looked like a scratch. But it's individual letters, see?"

The old man dropped the button in Smith's outstretched left hand and offered him the magnifying glass. The constable made his way to the window and studied the stamped wording. Once the text was enlarged, he could make out the words 'RYAN & SON EIRE'.

"Are they based in Ireland, Mr Davies?"

"No, lad! You're in luck, London! Go down the next street, look for their shop sign. I know them well. They are an Irish family, and it is definitely their name on the button. I think you might have found your next clue!"

The bobby left the magnifier on the table with a clatter and tipped his hat politely. Thanking Mr Davies as he dashed out of the shop in great haste, he left the smiling tailor to close the door behind him.

It was beginning to rain as Constable Smith strode along purposefully to the next street, the raindrops splashing on his face as he looked up, scanning the shop signs running high above his head. Towards the end of the road, there it was—Ryan & Sons. Looking down, Smith cursed under his breath. The shop seemed closed. There were no lights on inside. On closer inspection, in fact, it looked abandoned. Despondently, sensing his red-hot line of enquiry rapidly cooling, the constable knocked anyway. Nothing. He rapped his gloved knuckles harder against the door. Still nothing. In frustration, he gave a series of almighty knocks.

After a moment or two, he turned on his heels, deciding to ask a nearby shop about the story behind the Ryan's vacant premises. Then, there was a creak of a door, and a voice with a heavy Irish accent shouted:

"Oi! Come ye back. I was just putting me legs on."

Constable Smith spun around and put a spurt into his determined stride.

"Good afternoon, Sir. May I come in, please?"

"Well, you'd better, hadn't you? With this rain 'n all. I am Malachi. What's with the rush, then? Knocking then running off. That's what kids do. Not men of the law." said the man.

"I knocked for quite some time, Sir. I thought that the shop had been abandoned."

"No, me boy. I am here, and my family 'n all. We came through from Belfast before The Great Hunger. Me boys do the work now. I just tip in a wee bit here, and there."

"Sir, this button—"

Smith took it out of his pocket.

"Sir, would this button have come from your shop?"

Malachi chuckled.

"Ooh, yes, lad. Yes, it was our 'n alright. They were rare, see. This batch came out with three leaves. After that, they only embossed 'em with four—for good luck like."

"Sir, would you still have records of purchasing these buttons?"

"Oh, no. We never kept records for buying 'em. It was cash on the hip for these. But I remember who the buyers were. After a customer's been for a fitting, I remember every inch of 'em up here," said Malachi tapping his temple. "Now, there were seven customers that year who wanted those buttons. It was when they were having some troubles over there back home—so it was like, mmm—like a show of patriotism, you could say. See the Irish were striving for independence. Well, some of them were. The Unionists—"

Constable Smith knew that it would be a long day if he did not speed things up.

"—Sir, please give me the list of names."

"Right you are. This isn't time for a history lesson is it, Constable. Now, let me see—"

Malachi stroked his chin as he stared up towards the ceiling. Smith's impatience was becoming more difficult to contain as he bit his tongue. The young constable pulled out his notepad and a pencil to keep himself distracted.

Malachi made a great show of remembering the names, with lengthy pauses in between. Eventually, he called out the fifth name that got Smith scribbling with glee.

"Elijah Sheehan. Now, he were a little vagabond. Not often I have no time for me own kind—but him—I often wished somebody would just kick the little swine in his head and make the world a better place. Always wanted to look the dandy, bloody lunatic. He didn't have two ha'pennies to rub together. Said it would go well with some snazzy shoes he had got from somewhere. Ideas above his station, you might say, when it came to his dress sense. He's a wrong 'un alright. What's he gone and done?"

Malachi didn't get an answer. Constable Smith tore back to the police station as fast as his legs would carry him.

"We got him, guv! We got him. Elijah Sheehan had a coat made with buttons just like this at Malachi Ryan's shop, down near Savile Row."

"Excellent, my man, excellent," said Chief Inspector Mason. "Now, we need to go and find Elijah. Finding the story behind the button was perhaps the easy part. A man can disappear in those slums and never be found if he has the right friends."

"Sir, I need another three men—plainclothes men, Sir. Get them visiting the boozers Sheehan frequents, for starters." advised the constable.

"Certainly, Smith. Choose who you want, and let me know your progress. I will go and see Clifford Iverson and update him."

The two officers left the station, keen that the investigation was making progress. The net was tightening around Elijah, and they were glad about that.

"Good afternoon, Sir." Greeted Chief Inspector Mason on Clifford Iverson's doorstep.

"Inspector," replied the surprised widower, before inviting Mason into the parlour.

"Mr Iverson, we believe we can tie Elijah Sheehan to your wife's abode. We found a distinctive button from a coat that seems to belong to him when we searched Camilla's flat. The bedroom to be precise."

Clifford shook his head. He couldn't believe what he heard. *After all the trouble she had caused with her infidelity she had actually invited him back into her bed again. Well, it seems she provoked the Lord's wrath once too often.*

"Did you make an inventory of your wife's missing possessions for us, Mr Iverson?"

"Yes, Sir. Here you go. I've added some detailed descriptions to each piece. That should help you pin down whether any jewellery that comes to light is hers or not."

Chief Inspector Mason perused the list thoughtfully.

"Were all these pieces custom made for your wife?"

"Yes. More fool me. And the silvery jewellery box. It was a French antique. The little musical mechanism worked perfectly. I had Camilla's name engraved on it. It was a birthday gift."

"Mr Iverson, anything that has a name engraved on it is very difficult to fence. The newspapers are full of the news of your wife's murder. Nobody will touch any of those items, not even the dodgiest of dealers. Equally, Sheehan won't want to hold onto it for long though. I expect he might try and scrape off the lettering, or disguise it in some way. We just need to wait until he offers it to one of our informers."

Clifford, cut to the bone with the news that Camilla was seeing that rogue at her posh pad in Mayfair, couldn't reply. A nod of his head was the best he could manage.

"Sir, Sheehan is going to make a mistake. Men like him always do. They get desperate for money and take a risk. We will find out, and we will arrest him. I have three plainclothes men on the beat looking for the scoundrel. We know the pubs he likes to visit, and the fences that are good at shifting a bit of jewellery. I will be back if I have any more news."

Clifford nodded again. He didn't stand up to shake the inspector's hand. Feeling defeated, he stayed mournful in his chair and raised his arm instead.

Elijah had found some basic lodgings in the middle of the Tyndall Slum. The peelers were too scared to put a foot into its overcrowded labyrinth of streets and alleys. A few weeks back, one bobby who had foolishly forgotten his whistle was nearly beaten to death for a bit of entertainment by the ruffians there. That vicious attack made it the perfect time for Sheehan to rest his murderous head in Tyndall. *Lady Luck has smiled on me, so she has.* Somebody at the parrot said the Irishman could sleep in an alcove under a big staircase and he had grabbed the opportunity. He spent the majority of his time holed up there.

He was doing badly, suffering longer and longer bouts of sobriety which drove him up the wall. Desperately uncomfortable, he felt like bugs were crawling under his flesh. Perspiration beaded and trickled down his grubby skin. Every cell in his body screamed for alcohol. Engulfed by a depression so deep, he never wanted to climb out of the darkness as he lay under the stairs. He could not afford to eat, and he had become so thin he was looking positively skeletal.

When it was dark, he would put on his posh clothes and try to find a way to get a drink. That was proving tricky. Of course, he had the jewels and the box which was worth a large fortune, but nobody would touch them. He did a bit of labouring and some begging. He tried his hand at pickpocketing when he got really desperate, although being caught stealing off other slum dwellers was likely to incur a savage beating.

He had heard from some of the lads at the shipyard that there would be a French ship in from Marseilles for a few days needing some repairs. Perhaps he could convince one of its hapless sailors to buy the items and sell them overseas where they would not be traced. Being French, they wouldn't be reading the newspaper. He was desperate now. *If somebody offers me ten quid, they can take the lot.*

Lacking cash and fearful, he hadn't been to his regular drinking holes since he decided to lie low and work out his next move, which was a pity for Sheehan—they were the only fellas he knew who would stump up and buy him a drink.

He walked through Tyndall. It was cold with a black sky spitting rain. He could have headed for any boozer, but against all instincts, he made for the Blue Parrot. It had been some days since the murder was discovered. *Surely, the coppers would have collared me by now if they had any hard evidence?* He felt the incriminating jewellery box in his coat pocket and gave a nervous swallow. Giving himself a pep talk, he decided they must be off his case by now, and looking elsewhere for Camilla's murderer.

Still, deciding it might be too risky to go in the pub itself, he decided to sneak to the back alley, planning to get a mate's attention when they came to use the privy. *Surely one of the boys can bring me a bottle or two to the gloomy alley?*

The streets were miserable that night with folk in huddles trying to keep warm. Stood around street fires, made in old metal barrels, their glowing faces laughed and cursed. The lonely figure of Sheehan walked towards a man drinking from a bottle.

"Be a good bloke and give me a bit of a taster?"

The group looked at him and began to laugh. He could still hear them when he turned into the next street.

"Yer off yer head, Charlie," shouted somebody after him.

Elijah walked around a small bend in the alleyway, and under a tunnel bridge. It seemed as though the dingy walls were alive. The black silhouettes of people moved against the walls, but nobody spoke. It was eerie. He panicked and began to run. He ran all the way to the Blue Parrot and collapsed in the alleyway, breathless.

A tart came out with a punter.

"Darlin'," he gasped in the slickest way he could. "Please ask Jacky to come out the back here. Tell him it's an old friend fallen on hard times, sweetheart."

"Can't you see I'm busy?" she tutted, before addressing the more pressing needs of her customer.

Still, the girl must have had a heart of gold because once she performed her business, she went back inside and sent Jacky right out to see him.

"Elijah, where have you been mate? We worried ourselves sick. We thought they put you in the nick, but we heard nothing on the grapevine from the regulars in there. We didn't know what the hell was going on with you since the—"

"—look, Jacky, I'm in a bit of a tight spot. Bit short of cash, that's all. I've got some stuff to fence—worth a small bloody fortune. I'll be tip-top when I have shifted that."

"Stop right there, Elijah! If that's what I think it is, nobody wants that gear of yours. You vanished when the news of that Camilla sort's murder came to light. I reckon your little nest egg has something to do with that former posh bird of yours. Throw it in the bloody river, or you are bound to hang."

"Do you think I can come in, Jacky? It's raw out here?" begged Elijah.

"Nah. If the coppers see you with us, we'll all be in it then, mate. We don't want our collars felt because of you."

A desperate Sheehan gave him his best begging look, hoping to melt his pal's heart. He kept staring at Jacky in the eye until he gave in.

> "Tell ya what—what if we club together, and buy you a nice bottle to warm the old cockles. Then you can get off the streets? Drink it somewhere nice?"

> "Awe, Jacky, that will be great, just great. You're a smashing bloke. Ta."

Elijah waited in anticipation. He couldn't wait to rip the cap off and pour the bottle of booze down his throat. Keen to keep a low profile, Jacky sent the girl out with the bottle. It was cheap but kicked like a mule. Elijah had drunk half the bottle by the time he reached the street fire that he had passed earlier.

> "Look what I got me, ya bye-blows!" he laughed as he staggered along, waving the bottle in the air.

He tried to tell them something else but couldn't get the words in the right order. Walking straight was proving to be a delightful challenge for the Irishman, and he felt good because of it.

He decided that he would save the remainder of the bottle for the next day, but he kept on taking another mouthful. Each time, he promised himself it would be the last swig, but persistently weakened. Eventually, as he put the bottle to his lips one 'final' time, he was dismayed to realise that he had drunk it all.

Elijah woke up the next morning, still a bit tipsy, thinking the world was full of promise. That feeling was soon to fade. He had been using his coat as a pillow. Last night he had not folded it very well, and a sleeve with its cuff buttons was uppermost. As he propped himself up, feeling a little worse for wear, he noted that his good coat had a missing button. *What a bloody disaster. I'll have to find a new one. Them buttons are bobby dazzlers. Dunno how I'll pay for it, mind.*

The damp hole under the staircase was becoming as unwelcoming as a prison cell. There was constant traffic going up and down the stairs giving him no peace at all. Thud. Thud. Thud. Each step roared in his head as his simmering temper began to boil over. As night fell, he became more and more tempted to go down to the Blue Parrot.

That night, Elijah was braver. *Everything had gone fine the evening before. The heat was surely off by now? The Parrot would be Mason's focus for me, so it would.* He slunk down to the pub, in better spirits than the night before. As he opened the door, the warm, putrid smell of beer and spirits hit him first, then the body odour. *Ahh. I'm home.*

The atmosphere was particularly jolly that night. There was a small band of musicians playing a cheerful tune, Irish by the sounds of it. A fiddle, accordion, and flute made up the trio. Everyone was clapping their hands or stomping their feet in time with the music. Some sang, although not all in tune. A handful of women were dancing in the middle of the floor with a circle of men leering at them, wondering who they might go out the back with.

Elijah spotted Jacky in the corner at the rear of the pub and waved.

"Hello mate," said Jacky, looking shiftily around, hoping no one saw them together.

"Hello Jacky," grinned Elijah. "This looks like a real good knees-up tonight, eh?"

"Can I buy you a beer?"

"Lord above, Jacky. Thought you'd never ask. But make it a whiskey, eh?"

Elijah gave Jacky a hearty and thankful slap on the back, a jolt so hard, Jacky spilt some of his pint. He stared down at the tiny puddle, irritated that some of his precious ale had been wasted. *Still, it's good to see old Sheehan, I suppose.*

"That ship's in from Marseilles," said Jacky, secretively.

"How do ya know that?"

"Some Frogs over in the corner there," answered Jacky quietly, tipping his head in their direction. "Tough buggers them 'uns."

Waving his hand in the air, Jacky raised his voice:

"Hey!" he shouted, his arm moving erratically. "Hey! Four shots of whiskey over here, please, Daisy. Be a love, we're parched over here!"

Elijah knocked back a shot and pondered the situation for a short while. Things were only getting better and better. He felt the angular corners of the box in his coat and started to pluck up the courage to approach the French mariners. As he gave some more thought about what his approach should be, he threw back a few more tots of rum to oil the cogs of his devious little mind. Then, after a determined slap of his hand on the bar, and a knowing grin to Jacky, he sauntered over to the table where the Frenchmen were sitting. Jacky looked on, guiltily, glad to be free of his toxic friend.

The two men looked rough. They were very big for Frenchmen. Elijah arrogantly sat down on the bench next to them.

"Bon-jew-er Mu-shew-urs," he said, the only French he knew.

They stared at him without smiling, annoyed by his interruption.

"Bonjour," was the eventual response, delivered in a thick French accent.

Elijah couldn't offer them a beer to smooth the path to the sale as he had no money. With no other choice, he subtly got to the point, hoping they spoke more English than he did French.

"I am a jewellery merchant," he said.

The men nodded their heads and continued sipping their pints. Elijah thought he had confused them, so he tried again slowly, with simpler words.

"I—sell—gifts—for—women? You want?"

Nothing. *Please let them understand me. Come on!* With the crossed fingers of his left hand in his pocket stroking one of the corners of the antique box, he continued.

"Perhaps you want to buy your lover a little gift for being a good girl while you have been away?" said Elijah suggestively.

The two men laughed and nodded their heads. *Aha! They do understand.* Elijah prepared to get into his stride, his full charm offensive developing.

"You will be very lucky men with your women when you get home if you get them a nice English souvenir," he continued, believing the titillating ideas were appealing to the foreigners.

"You steal eet, oui?"

"Nah! Nah, fellas. I come from Birmingham. Up north—the, er, Jewellery Quarter. I come to sell all the beautiful things here in London," explained Elijah, grasping for a story that sounded authentic. "Only the French know about true beauty. That's why I wanted to talk to you."

All three men gave a belly laugh. Elijah was pleased his nervousness didn't show in his.

"I will show you something. But not in here, too many people. Don't want to get hit over the head by some ruffian for my troubles, now do I? Let me check the coast is clear."

Elijah got up from the bench and walked toward the back door that opened onto the alley. He glanced about furtively. *Great, there's nobody here.* He knew he ran the risk of the French men robbing him, but he was so desperate, he was prepared to take his chances. He beckoned them over with a grin and a wave of his arm.

He put his hand inside his greatcoat pocket, fumbled within the box and pulled out the locket he robbed from Camilla's flat. He showed it to the French men. He allowed them to look at the thing but not touch it, in case they pulled a fast one and stole it.

Elijah was delighted seeing them utterly captivated as they peered at the glittering jewel in the gloom. *The deal's in the bag here. I feel it in my old Irish bones. They're on the hook. Just gotta reel 'em in. Plenty of drink for me tonight, methinks!*

"But eet ees dark 'ere, Monsieur."

Elijah, convinced they were alright blokes, walked to the street in front of the pub, and stood under a bright cone of lamplight where they could get a better look at it. The Irishman dangled the jewel, and it swivelled round and around. It was the most beautiful golden locket encrusted with blue sapphires and sparkling white diamonds.

Suddenly, Sheehan realised his trust had been misplaced. Grabbed by the throat and thrust against the wall by one of the huge men, he was choked until he released his grasp on the necklace. He raised his hands and tried to pull the big brute's paw off his windpipe, with his eyes bulging and breath rasping. He didn't care about losing the necklace anymore. Losing his life was a far more pressing concern. *Besides, I still have some more things to sell.*

"Take it, lads. It's yours. A gift from England." he whimpered.

The big hand's grip on Elijah's throat was unrelenting, despite one of the Frenchmen playing with the newly pilfered necklace. His face a mix of awe and pride. With defiance, he stared at Sheehan in the eye as the scrawny Irishman clawed away, trying to free himself.

"Yes, sergeant," he announced in a loud English voice, "Looks like we have found our man. He has the goods alright. And look, he has a missing button that matches the one we found on his coat sleeves."

Constable Smith stepped from out of the shadows. He patted down Sheehan and felt the antique box. After dragging it out from the deep inside pocket, the officer traced his finger along the engraved name.

"You are under arrest, Elijah Sheehan for the murder of Mrs Camilla Iverson," announced Constable Smith, his face glowing with pride as well as the lamplight.

Sheehan knew it was all over for him. *The game's up.* People were inquisitive, and soon the sloshed patrons of the pub were in the street watching the action. Eager to save face, Elijah shouted abuse:

"You've got the wrong man, I tell ya! You plods are going to regret this!"

He threw a few loose punches into thin air and made a huge scene. The small, weak man's threats and bravado impressed no one. It would be the alcohol that Elijah Sheehan had so desperately craved that had betrayed him to the coppers, and now he was going to jail. A paddy wagon appeared through the throng, and Elijah was put into the cage. There was another bitter but pointless struggle as he was detained.

"You're going to be eating porridge for a while, mate. I would behave if I were you!" advised Constable Smith.

The next morning, Chief Inspector Mason paid a visit to Clifford Iverson. The man looked haggard, and the officer felt sorry for him as he updated him on the latest developments.

"This sordid mess will be in the newspapers by this evening," said Iverson.

"I am sorry, Sir."

"So am I! so am I!" mumbled Clifford. "It's my sons. They are going to be humiliated by this."

"Nobody has to know about the affair, Sir."

"I told you. I might have kept the divorce out of the papers with some backhanders and favours, but that doesn't stop the men's tongues wagging. They are worse than washerwomen. It will flare up again. Topic of the week over a pint, no doubt. Her selfishness ruined everything for our family. I should have bloody strangled her myself. Sheehan will tell everything to the court, his doomed final moments in the spotlight—and this time, I doubt I can keep the journalists from reporting it."

"How long until the trial?" asked Clifford.

"No longer than three weeks, Sir, he has confessed to murdering her, and he shows no regret for his actions. He will hang."

"Do I need to be in the court?" asked Clifford.

"No, Sir. You were not married to the woman, and we can ask the jewellers to confirm the custom pieces were made for Mrs Iverson."

"Chief Inspector, can you please provide me with any documentation I will need to sign? The only thing I can do for my sons is to take them as far away from London as possible. I am booking a passage for us to America imminently. It will be possible for me to establish some new shipyards there. We need a new start, and America needs ships to carry its growing exports across the Atlantic."

"I understand, Sir. I am sorry I could not do more to lighten your burden."

"Thank you, Inspector. I appreciate everything you have done to catch that rotter."

Elijah Sheehan was hanged at dawn on a Wednesday morning. He was unremorseful until the bitter end. Nobody came to say goodbye. He was offered a last meal but requested a last bottle, not unusual for the class of criminal he was.

He whistled on his way to the gallows, making jokes as he went along. Nobody would ever know whether it was out of ignorance or fear. When asked by the hangman if he had any last words, Elijah Sheehan's answer was 'no'.

19

DINNER AT EIGHT

Fate had dealt a far better hand for Ebba, the only surviving Sheehan. By now, she was almost qualified. She had flourished as a student and was always in the top ten of her class. She did not know if she would specialise in anything particular yet. Currently, she was assisting in surgical operations. It was almost the dawning of the twentieth century, and there was great experimentation with new medical technology.

She was doing her internship at the Royal London, which was a training hospital. The hours were long, and a lot of the cases were heartbreaking. As she progressed towards her degree, it was positive to see that the rivalry between male and female students was starting to diminish. Respect had begun to develop based on the capabilities of the doctor rather than their gender, amongst the medical community at least. The wider population still preferred to be treated by a male doctor.

In Ebba's mind, the high-profile trial and execution of her father threatened to derail her progress. Being a female doctor was hard enough without the shame of the case wearing down upon her soul. Back then, picking up on her sense of foreboding, it was Jessica who finally sat her down and gave her a talking to.

> "Ebba, we do not choose our parents. We get what we get. You can choose to let this eat you alive, or you can continue living as you always have, that is without even a shadow of Elijah in your life. Stop reading the newspapers, and don't listen to the gossip. There is nothing that you can change by worrying. Elijah sealed his own fate, lass. He was an evil man, always looking after number one. Do not allow yourself to take him into your future with you."

It took a few days for Ebba to process the speech, but she heeded Jessica's advice. Soon, Elijah was not even a pin-prick on the horizon. She had also discussed it with Molly, who was now the closest person she had to a sibling.

> "Oh Ebba," she consoled her. "Listen to Jessica. She is wise. You have a life of joy ahead of you. You survived your father's abuse and abandonment. Come on now, cheer up," she said, before giving her friend a hug.

Ebba didn't look too convinced, her weak, thin smile betraying her.

"Ebba, did I ever tell you about my Uncle Charlie who died on the floor outside the privy. Like your pa, he was an evil man. Never worked a day and drank his insides clean away. Everyone was so used to him falling over dead drunk, that when he did, they left him lying out there for a whole day before they noticed he had kicked the bucket. My aunt realised there was something wrong when she walked past at nigh on midnight and put the boot into his ribs and he didn't stir. She swore like a docker dragging him onto the street to get his body collected."

Sensing the tension easing, Ebba and Molly laughed until they cried.

"Ya see, Ebba, every family has a tale to tell. You're nothing special, my girl. But you don't tell a soul about poor old Charlie. You hear me?"

Ebba still had very little to do with the McAlistair family and moved like a ghost about their house. She did not intrude on any of their social gatherings. She used the servant's facilities, ate in the kitchen if she was back in time for a meal, and helped out below stairs where she could. The staff had not changed apart from the fact they had all grown a little older, and perhaps Mr Carrington and Mrs Shaw had both softened a little in their starchy demeanours. Ebba fondly remembered the incident with Betty's cast off blue dress all those years ago. It was another story she and Molly often reminisced about. There was a concerted effort by the butler and the housekeeper to protect and nurture the junior staff where possible, and the camaraderie beneath the stairs was noteworthy.

Ebba and Molly had just been discussing their adventures when Ebba received a message in her room that Mrs McAlistair wanted to speak to her. She bounced down the four flights of stairs and into the parlour where Mrs McAlistair awaited her arrival. After tentatively knocking, she entered the room.

"Good day, Mrs McAlistair."

"Ah, Ebba, my dear," said her benefactor in her most sophisticated tone. "I don't know if you are informed, but Elliot Chadwick is in London, and he will be dining with us tomorrow night at eight o'clock as usual. Will you please join us?"

"Thank you for the invitation, I shall be delighted to attend." smiled Ebba.

"That will be all." said Mrs McAlistair with a hint of a smile.

Ebba floated out of the room with decorum, then rushed back to the kitchen via the servant's corridors.

"I am invited to dinner with the family tomorrow evening," she said with glee. The housekeeper looked at her and smiled. "Don't worry Mrs Shaw, I can afford my own dress this time."

The whole kitchen burst into laughter, including the housekeeper and butler. Molly was even more excited about the invitation than Ebba.

"For heaven's sake, Molly, I am not going to the Ritz, I am going to the McAlistair's dining room. I would prefer to stay here. Do you know that I have only seen the inside of the house proper three times? Once when I arrived here, that time I was invited to dinner, which was so long ago, I can't remember, and just now for the next invitation."

"How should we do your hair?" asked Molly.

Mrs Shaw had given her the afternoon off to get Ebba ready for the evening.

"Just let it hang," said Ebba.

"No!" shrieked Molly. "This is the closest I will ever come to fine dining, so you will look good on my behalf."

Ebba laughed.

"Okay, Molly. Do as you like. I won't stop you."

Ebba had spoilt herself with a dress a few years back. She had seen it hanging in a ladies boutique and asked for the price. It was far too expensive for her pocket, so she, and Molly bought similar fabric and lace, and made a copy of it together over a series of long winter's evenings. It was designed to make an impression, and it did. The skirt was a deep rich plum colour, and the bodice was gold lace. The sleeves draped off the shoulder. The unlined lace along the top of the dress gave it a sensual feminine appeal.

> "I don't want my hair to be a mass of horrid ringlets everyone insists on wearing," said Ebba with a smile, ducking as her hand batted Molly's curling iron away.

Obeying the instruction to the letter, Molly only put a gentle curl in the longer lengths of Ebba's locks and then arranged her hairstyle off her face with a pretty silver clip. Ebba was a natural beauty, and she didn't need anything else. She was dazzling as she was. When she came down the stairs into the kitchen, the staff cheered.

> "Look at you, Ebba. Pretty as a picture," said Mrs Shaw, as the rest of the staff clapped.

Escorted by the butler, Ebba walked into the drawing room, all smiles. A hush fell over the room for a moment, and then the conversation slowly began again. Mr Carrington poured her a tot of sherry in a small crystal glass.

She greeted Mr and Mrs McAlistair first, then she worked her way around the room. Arthur and Betty had married a few years back, and neither of them looked any cheerier for it. Betty looked Ebba over from top to bottom and greeted her coolly. Richard was engaged to a lovely young lady called Rose, and they both received

Ebba with genuine sincerity. When she got to Arthur, he took her hand.

"My oh my," he whispered in hushed tones." It is no wonder mother insists you use the servant's quarters. You would be way too much of a diversion for my father."

With his head still by her ear, he laughed wickedly. She tried to remove her hand from his, but he would not let go. It was so subtle that no one would have noticed even if they were watching.

"We will see each other again, won't we Ebba?" he grinned, her skin crawling as he impinged on her personal space.

Ebba was at a loss for words. It was not that she did not know how to take care of herself. She was a trainee doctor, and she worked with a lot of different, challenging personalities in challenging circumstances. No, it was his suggestive approach that was so unexpected, more so given he was within yards of his wife. Feeling her skin crawl, she firmly twisted her hand from his grasp and went to find someone with whom she could quickly strike up a conversation.

Elliot eventually had the opportunity to greet Ebba. He never gave it thought that she would be a woman now. He always remembered her as a little girl. Her face was radiant. Her hair flowed in silky waves down her back, and the tight-fitting bodice of her dress gave a hint to what lay beneath. He was dumbfounded that this was the urchin he saved so many years back.

She watched him cross the room. He was tall, definitely over six feet, and now in his mid-twenties. His striking dark brown hair was cut neatly, and his cleanly shaven face sported a strong jaw. He was immaculate, no longer the boyish Elliot she remembered. He was most definitely a man.

He stood in front of her and took her hand. She had spent years studying the anatomy of the human body, but there was nothing in the textbooks that explained the reaction her body was having to his hand. It felt like an electric current was flowing between them. She blushed at her thoughts, as she felt him pick up on her shy attraction.

"You are beautiful," were his first words to her.

She looked into his eyes and smiled.

"You're just saying that because you have seen me at my worst when you found me on the street," she laughed nervously.

He did not break the gaze. His expression was so alluring, she felt herself hold her breath.

"Oh, I'm not so sure about that," he said as he squeezed her hand with affection, and kissed her on the cheek.

His confidence intimidated her, and eventually, she broke off eye contact.

Before they could say any more to each other, the dinner gong sounded. Elliot gave Ebba his arm and escorted her to the table. Much to Elliot's disappointment, they were not seated next to each other. Ebba was placed between Arthur and Richard. The dining table was decorated with the finest silver candelabras and extravagant bunches of flowers, making it a little difficult to see anything but the other guests' faces hovering above the ostentatious display.

"Elliot, you are still studying at Harvard, are you not? How are you enjoying Massachusetts?" asked George McAlistair.

"It is a tremendous university, thank you, Sir," replied Elliot.

"The most advanced in the world, I believe?" the old man continued.

"Oh yes, the technology they are developing is going to make a difference to thousands, perhaps millions of people."

"How so?" asked Betty.

"Well, I am specialising in pulmonary—err, breathing diseases," answered Elliot with passion as he looked around at the sea of heads. "Most lung disease can be reduced—"

"—oh!" Betty said, looking down her nose at him as she rudely interrupted. "You mean like black lung in coal miners?"

"Yes. Precisely that sort of thing." Elliot was glad she understood. "Those terrible conditions can be eliminated if large companies choose to work alongside university academics."

"Daddy owns a coal mine in Wales," she pouted.

"Then, I would like to meet him. He would be very interested in all this, I'm sure," replied Elliot.

"Well, I am not so sure about that, Elliot. Daddy says the job is what it is, illness and all. I am sure the men use black lung as an excuse to work less."

Everything went silent. Ebba could not believe what she was hearing from the mouth of this spoilt upper-class woman. *Betty has obviously never seen a suffering patient with chronic lung disease fighting for breath.*

"Betty, this condition affects hundreds of thousands of men. Do you have any of your own ideas to address this issue?" Elliot probed. "It is important to keep these highly-skilled, highly-productive men in the workforce, is it not?"

"We cannot wait around for every man to recuperate from black lung. It is preferable to replace them with new men. That—is my opinion."

Every eye was on Elliot and Betty. Blithely, Betty continued eating as if she had just looked out of the window and described the weather outside. Elliot, on the other hand, had put his cutlery down and was looking straight at her.

Sensing attention was on the awkward simmering argument, Arthur put his right hand on Ebba's knee and started pulling up her skirt. She tried to push his arm away, but she could not do it without causing a scene. He was very strong and tensed his muscles in defiance, leaving his hand locked in position. Ebba could not wriggle from his grip. She felt his fingertips walking on her knee, pulling up more and more her skirt. She wished she had bought a thicker, less flimsy fabric to make the dress, but her funds did not allow. Now, she was deeply regretting that decision.

> "Daddy says that if the government implements any regulations regarding miner's health, he will just fire them all, and hire men who need the money more."

She picked up her napkin and wiped her pouting lips elegantly

Arthur's hand was now fully under Ebba's skirt, and moving up her thigh. She was squirming to get away, keeping her upper body as motionless as possible. He glanced across to his right, with a stare that told her he knew she wanted it to stop but could do nothing about it without causing an embarrassing scene.

Elliot was incensed. The consummate medical professional was past the point of being polite when confronted by Betty's latest selfish comment. He was downright disgusted with her and everyone could see it. All those around the table were drawn into the gravity of the conversation, their eyes on Elliot, awaiting his riposte.

Arthur started to stroke Ebba's bare thigh skin suggestively, his hand moving closer and closer toward her hip.

"I am sure Daddy says a lot of things, my dear, but this is what I say—a man gets paid to do his job, not to give his life."

Nobody had seen that reply coming, and George McAlistair sensed the need to deviate from the topic as fast as possible.

Arthur's fingers were at the top of Ebba's thigh now, and if it had not been for George McAlistair's diplomacy, Arthur would have put his hand where it definitely shouldn't be.

"Mr Carrington," he said loudly, "please pass me the condiments."

The butler had to lean in between Ebba and Arthur to get to them. Anticipating the interruption, Arthur slid his arm back before the butler could see what he had been up to. Ebba seized the opportunity to flee and jumped to her feet.

"Can you please excuse me from the table, Mr McAlistair, I am suddenly feeling very ill. I have a terrible headache and feel nauseous," she croaked, as her shamed voice gave out on her.

She stood up anxiously, and without waiting to be excused, fled from the room. The carefree, relaxed evening was transformed into a fragile, icy atmosphere where, with one slight vibration, everything could shatter into pieces.

Elliot was disappointed of course. He had been looking forward to seeing Ebba tremendously and was concerned that she was feeling ill. She had seemed well enough earlier, so he didn't think it would be too much of an imposition to enquire about her health later.

"Let us go to the smoking room, gentlemen," said Mr McAlistair after the meal. "I am sure that the ladies have plenty to discuss."

They all stood up from the table. Elliot approached Mrs McAlistair quietly.

"Ma'am, I am very worried about Ebba. Could you arrange that I see her, please?"

"Oh, Elliot. Don't worry about that girl. She will be fine in the morning. You know young women.

They can feel off so very quickly. You are a doctor—you should know what I am referring to."

"Oh, Mrs McAlistair, I would feel so responsible for any upset she may cause in your home. It may be something contagious. It could be very dangerous. It is better to be safe than sorry, is it not? A headache, nausea and a sore throat are the first signs of scarlet fever," said Elliot, playing the idiot, hoping his hostess would capitulate. "It's quite prevalent at the moment."

Mary McAlistair's eyes grew wider, sensing she was being spun a yarn, but agreed to save face.

"You do have a point. Better safe than sorry, Elliot. Yes, you may see her."

She rang a little silver bell, and the butler appeared.

"Mr Carrington, please take Dr Chadwick to Miss Sheehan's room. He is concerned that she is suffering from something that may be contagious."

"Yes, Ma'am. Sir, please follow me."

As Elliot shadowed the butler up the servant's staircase, Arthur sidled up to his mother.

"What was that all about?" asked Arthur.

"Oh, Elliot is worried the girl might have something contagious."

"Yes. That is a good idea, Mother. The servant's quarters are rather cramped, and things spread easily there. By the way, what did you say Ebba's surname is?"

"Sheehan, Ebba Sheehan."

Before Arthur joined the men in the smoking room, Betty pulled her husband to one side.

"Arthur, isn't it time we moved out of your mother's house? We've been here years as man and wife. Can't we have a home of our own, like other married couples?" whined Betty, standing in front of the mirror above the fireplace, gazing at herself.

"Not this again," tutted Arthur. "It is convenient here. Everything is provided for. The house is well run. We don't have the bother of hiring servants—and it costs pennies compared to paying for this all ourselves."

"Money is not the issue, Arthur. We have plenty of it."

"Well, what is bothering you, my darling?"

"It seems that your mother and father are beginning to mix with a class of person lower than I am accustomed to. I really did not enjoy that little scene that Elliot made at the table. Who does that good-for-nothing pipsqueak think he is!"

"Yes, he was a bit difficult about it all. Who cares about miners anyway? The ones I have met in passing at your father's mine seem happy with their lot," answered Arthur.

"Oh, my love. We don't need a big home like this yet. Maybe just a nice flat. Mayfair is a wonderful address, you know. Let's start looking tomorrow."

"Of course, of course," said Arthur curiously accommodating to his wife's wishes for once.

But his mind wasn't on buying property—it was imagining Ebba's writhing naked body under his, while his wife lay sleeping.

20

THE EARLY RETIREMENT

Elliot knocked on Ebba's door. Panicked, thinking it might be Arthur, she did nothing.

"Come on. Open up, Ebba. It's me, Elliot," he whispered.

Ebba opened the door with reluctance and stood guarding the threshold to her room. Wet tears of humiliation streaked her face and made it puffy.

"What on earth is wrong?" he asked as he stroked her hair off her face. He put his arms around her, inviting her to rest her head on his chest. Tentatively, she did so. She could hear his strong heartbeat intertwined with the deep rumble of his voice as he spoke.

"Don't worry. It's probably something I ate. I am not used to shellfish. I felt so violently ill I had to leave the table. Perhaps it was that?"

"Come now. Let me take a look at you, as a professional," he pleaded.

"No, Elliot. Really, I am fine!" she protested

He whispered in her ear:

"Can I remind you I am a doctor?"

"So am I," she smiled.

He nuzzled his head in her hair and didn't want to let her go. He held her a little longer. It seemed so natural. She felt safe, comfortable, and was glad he didn't let go immediately.

"Come inside," she asked politely. "I have a chair and a bed. I can't offer you tea though."

"Well, since you are the one convalescing you take the bed, and I'll take the chair." smiled Elliot

Molly had heard about her early departure via Mr Carrington and knocked on Ebba's door.

"It's me, Molly. Can I come in?"

"Yes," called Ebba.

Molly peered through the gap in the door and saw Ebba lying in her bed.

"What on earth are you doing in bed so early?" she asked, seeing Ebba fully clothed in her beautiful dress, tear streaks on her face. "What has happened? You look a sight for sore eyes!"

She dashed to the bedside to be closer to her friend, then saw Elliot.

"Oh, so sorry. I didn't see you there. You must be Dr Chadwick. Is Ebba alright? She doesn't look very good at all," said Molly with concern.

"Elliot, meet my good friend Molly. She works here for the McAlistair's."

"Is this 'the Elliot' from the coffin house?"

The others didn't know to whom Molly's question was directed, but in unison Elliot and Ebba answered 'yes'. At that, they all started laughing. Molly gained her composure first.

"Tell you what, you two, I'm going to run down to the kitchen and brew up some tea. You both look like you need a cuppa."

Molly tripped over Ebba's bedside rug in her haste to leave, grinned around the door, then disappeared as quickly as she had arrived.

"She's a character," laughed Elliot. "You seem to look out for each other."

"Yes, she is a gem—has a heart of gold."

"How is your internship going?" asked Elliot.

"It's hard work studying, and working here at the same time, and they pay me tuppence for my effort, but I still love it. Being able to save a life is truly a gift from God."

"I feel the same way," agreed Elliot. "There are so many people that need help. Like I said at dinner, the plight of the coal miners concerns me most. There are very few consultants with knowledge of lung disease. I have some simple suggestions that may assist in preventing it, but it will be a challenge. I think Betty put it in the correct perspective. The mine bosses don't care. Plenty of young lads are ready to step into their dead pa's shoes. They have to support their families. There is no incentive to change how things work, from either viewpoint. I know some unscrupulous mine owners still secretly use child labour when they know the inspector won't be visiting for a while. What sort of life do they have?"

Ebba nodded her head.

"I am leaning towards general practice. It is a good position for a woman. It covers a lot of issues, both social, and medical, and a woman will always speak more freely to another woman. It also means I can help your parents at the coffin house. Will the medical corps be happy to send you to Wales, Elliot?"

"I did contact them, given the number of miners under their care and they have tentatively agreed. Ebba, we have an advantage over other doctors in that we know the poor, and we are comfortable with them. These rich fellows can't relate to the conditions the common folk have to live and work in."

It was an angle that Ebba had never considered. She felt embarrassed she had overlooked something so obvious.

"So yes, to answer your question, when I am finished at medical school, I am going to work in Wales."

Ebba felt disappointment wash over her.

"I thought you would choose somewhere closer—like Birmingham, perhaps."

"They have enough medical care there. Very few specialists want to move to Wales. There is not as much money to be made in the valleys, but there is a small practice run by another fellow who also specialises in pulmonary disease. He has offered to assist me in starting a clinic for the medical corps."

"I haven't even given thought to where I am going."

"You need to. You will be fully qualified soon." smiled Elliot.

Molly knocked on the door and came into the small room. Elliot stood up and helped her with the tea tray.

"My word, Ebba, the man is a gentleman, so he is. He is a good catch." She joked coyly. "He'll make someone a fine husband one day."

Elliot laughed spontaneously and sincerely.

"It is Ebba who will be the good catch," chuckled Elliot. "Beauty and brains will marry the brains and the beast."

Molly thought it was hilarious.

"I'm going to have to excuse myself. Mrs Shaw has a million and one things for us to do, clearing up after the dinner party. I am sure you have lots to talk about 'n all. I'll leave you with the doctor."

"Thank you, Molly," said Elliot kindly.

"Yes, thanks," smiled Ebba.

With that, Molly was gone, just sneaking Ebba a cheeky wink as she closed the door behind her.

Elliot loosened his tie and pulled his chair closer to the bed. Ebba was sitting upright, drinking her tea. He took her left hand and kissed it gently. The same electrifying surge coursed through her body as before.

"Will we always be friends, Elliot?"

"Best friends!" he replied.

"Are you always going to look out for me?"

"Always" he pledged, stroking the back of her hand.

The contrast between the way his loving touch felt and the unwanted carnal advances from Arthur earlier could not have been more pronounced.

They finished their tea together in comfortable silence, like they had many a time in the kitchen, back at the coffin house.

"I have to go now, Ebba. I'd better tell Mrs McAlistair that you are not suffering from a contagious disease."

Ebba laughed.

"When do you leave for America?"

"I sail tomorrow afternoon, at five o'clock. But I'll be back soon, I promise," answered Elliot.

"I can't see you off at the quayside because I am on duty at that time," said Ebba dismally.

They both stood up, knowing it was time for Elliot to leave. Just before he reached for the door handle, his curiosity and concern could no longer be contained.

"Ebba, I know that you were not ill this evening. Shocked, yes. Ill, no. Something upset you at the table. You can tell me anything—you do know that?"

"Of course," she answered a little too brightly. "I just felt a little out of sorts. I probably did my dress up a little too tightly. Silly me. Always looking to make a good impression with the well-to-do McAlistairs. The etiquette of those formal dinners is so frightful. As you say, we are people who know what it's like to be a commoner. The world of fine dining is very foreign to me."

She was glad, if guilty, that Elliot swallowed her white lie about her hurried escape from the dinner table.

They reached for the door handle together, and their fingers touched. He took her hand and kissed it again. Noticing Ebba's stunned but happy expression, Elliot took her into his arms and held her. He stroked her hair and face.

"You're my special girl, Ebba."

"I know," she answered.

With the thought of sailing away tomorrow weighing heavily on his mind, Elliot looked down at her and kissed her tenderly. The thought of being separated from her again hurt. He seized the moment, sensing his advances would not be spurned. He didn't exactly know what was going through his racing mind, but he suspected he was falling in love with the little urchin who had grown into a most beautiful woman. They broke apart and held a long, smouldering gaze. Reluctantly, Elliot stepped into the corridor.

"Goodnight, then, Miss Sheehan. Until next time," he whispered, as she quietly closed the door behind him.

The studying Elliot planned to do on the seven-day sail to Massachusetts was futile. All he could think of was Ebba—and the certainty in his heart that there was a future for them.

21

THE RETURN OF THE SCOUNDREL

Arthur's next unwanted imposition on Ebba would be in the early hours of Christmas Day that year. The staff had given themselves a small Christmas party in the kitchen, but Ebba who returned to the house way after midnight missed all the festivities. The night was drizzly and uncharacteristically warm for mid-winter.

It had been a long shift for newly qualified Dr Sheehan. The hospital was chaotic with all kinds of merrymaking gone wrong. Injuries due to domestic disputes, knife wounds, alcohol poisoning, dog bites. The list was endless, and remarkable, and continued until clocking off time. Later highlights were a man who had electrocuted himself, burning his hand severely, and a young child with a marble stuck up his nose.

Ebba was exhausted. She had been on shift for eighteen hours, and she did not think she could take another case when a nurse announced that a woman had come in with a broken arm.

"You have to see her, Dr Sheehan. I don't trust anybody else to cast that arm. She is very old, and the bone is very fragile. I am sure she will respond better to the gentle touch of a woman."

She handed the patient's details to Ebba.

"Sister, please allocate this case to another doctor. I am on my way home."

Breaking protocol, the equally tired sister handed the notes over anyway. Ebba shook her head dismissively as she looked down at the patient's notes in exasperation. Then suddenly, her expression changed. The patient's name was a familiar one: Bess Grantham.

"How old is this woman?" asked Ebba.

"About sixty. You can never tell, mind. She's from Spitalfields, they age quicker there."

Spitalfields was one of the most dangerous slums in London with the poorest of the poor living there. The area attracted migrants. This, in turn, led to the development of factions, which intensified the violence and added to the general hardship grinding impoverishment brought forth.

"I see. I'll take the case," said Ebba, and walked toward the ward where Bess Grantham was lying.

The nurse shook her head in bewilderment. Damned doctors, a law unto themselves! The patient was in obvious pain.

"Hello, Bess," said Ebba with compassion.

"Oh, doctor. The pain—oh, it is awful. Can you help me? Please?" begged Bess.

Bess was struggling so much, she didn't seem to recognise Ebba, but the girl recognised the elderly woman.

"I am going to give you a little bit of morphine to help stop the pain," advised Ebba. "How did this happen?"

"I slipped on the ice, Doctor."

"No, Bess. It's not cold enough tonight for a frost. How did this really happen?"

"Ah, a drunken lout ran me off me feet," she answered. "I don't want to make trouble. I don't think he meant to hurt me."

"I understand," said Ebba, with her best soothing bedside manner.

Ebba injected the morphine into Bess's arm with a large metal syringe and thick stainless-steel needle. Bess felt immediate relief. She was not fully sedated, but the pain was fading nicely.

"Nurse. Please sterilise the syringe and needle immediately," she ordered.

"Yes, Doctor."

"How do you know the slum?" asked Bess. "Did you work there? Sometimes the mission gets doctors in to look at us."

"No, Bess. I lived on the street for a while."

Ebba began to prepare to set the arm, as a woozy Bess looked at her face, trying to make sense of the comment.

"Bess, did you ever live in the Tyndall Slum?"

"Why yes, lass, donkey's years ago. But how do you know that world? Did you read about it in the paper?"

Ebba began setting the arm in a splint and bandaging it, making sure that the bones were correctly aligned, so they stood a chance of fusing back together.

"Oh, nothing like that. I was raised by a very kind neighbour. She had five daughters."

"Who were your parents? I lived there for years. For better, and for worse," she smiled.

"Do you remember Elijah and Sally Sheehan?"

Bess blinked with light-headedness. Her tongue began to loosen.

"Yes, a right pair they were the Sheehan's. Had a small girl. Curious name. Not a common one. Ella. No. Helen. Nah. Ebba, that's right. Ebba. I remember them now."

She took a closer look at the doctor's face, digging about in the recesses of her mind for where she knew it from.

"What is your name?"

"Well, Bess, I am Dr Ebba Sheehan," she answered, suddenly feeling very tearful. "I'm the child you saved all those years ago."

Bess couldn't believe what she was hearing. Ebba did everything she could to contain the tears. *Stiff upper lip time, Ebba. Come on. Keep a lid on this.* Despite her best efforts, one or two teardrops escaped, and she quickly wiped them away. Regardless of her age and her injury, the maternal instinct in Bess Grantham was as strong as ever.

"Aw lass," she whispered. "Now there, there. Don't cry. This is a joyful day," then Bess started to cry as well. "I can't believe it. We remembered you for years. We prayed for little Ebba every night. You must believe me. I thought you would be a goner, with Elijah being the way he was."

Bess looked at Ebba in utter disbelief, her good arm touching the doctor's shoulder to make sure she wasn't some sort of apparition.

"Me girls will be visiting here. They will not believe me if I tell them you're here, let alone a doctor. You have to make sure that ye are here to see them. We are all in Spitalfields, but they are good girls with good husbands, and families. Ebba, we are so blessed. Oh, thank the Lord that you survived."

"Yes, Bess, and today I can pay back a little of what I owe to you."

"You brought us joy, my girl. You never have to pay back anything to me."

"Bess, I am going to keep you here for a few days just to get that arm on the mend—and to see the girls too, I must admit. Let's have a cuppa and a catch up before I go home tonight?"

Bess nodded, too emotional to talk.

Ebba confided years of news with Bess over some steaming hot tea with extra sugar. The sweet liquid added the sparkle back to Mrs Grantham's eyes.

"You are the best Christmas gift I have ever had," said Ebba, choked with emotion.

"And you are mine, too."

"Now, you get some rest, Bess. I'll check on you soon."

An exhausted Mrs Grantham gave a wave before slipping into a deep, restful sleep.

Back in her room, Ebba collapsed on her bed but couldn't fall asleep. Her mind was too busy processing the odds of meeting Bess again after all these years. There were three soft knocks on the door. She was quite sure it was Molly being inquisitive about how the late shift had gone and to wish her a Merry Christmas. Relaxing in her nightclothes, she didn't bother to put on her dressing gown.

She unlocked the door, horrified to see Arthur McAlistair, rather than Molly in front of her. He was as drunk as a skunk, shirt almost unbuttoned to the waist, leaning against the door frame provocatively, he hoped.

He came into her room and closed the door. Ebba knew why he was there and what he wanted. She knew that if she panicked, he would take full physical advantage of her, but if she kept her wits, she could get out of the situation.

"I've come to wiiish you Merrry Chrisstmass, darllinng," slurred Arthur.

He'd uttered the type of empty platitude her useless lump of a father would have used on Sally before bedding her. She wanted to vomit at the thought of the eldest McAlister son coming near her.

"How sweet of you, Arthur," she answered with a big smile, hoping he couldn't see how false it was.

He moved closer to her. She could smell the alcohol on his breath, and he staggered a little when he moved. In his drunkenness, he had forgotten to lock the door behind him, and Ebba knew it. If she could just get around him, and out of the room, she would be home and dry. Unfortunately, that would mean flirting with him until he passed out. It was either that or risk being severely abused in a hasty drunken attack.

She moved towards him, sensually, smiling.

"I knew you would come over tonight, so I prepared a little." She smiled, twirling around him in her nightclothes as if giving him an erotic dance.

Arthur could not believe his good luck. It made him a bit dizzy, and he lost his balance. As he staggered, she pushed him as hard as she could, sending him sprawling backwards onto the bed, hitting his head against the wall. In an instant, Arthur had transitioned from dizzy to dazed.

Ebba ran from the room, slamming the door hard enough to alert Molly. Thank goodness, the plan worked. Aware that the noise could only indicate trouble with Arthur, Molly unlocked the door as fast as she could. Ebba put her forefinger to her lips to indicate that Molly needed to be quiet. Once safely inside, she closed the door softly and locked it behind her.

Ebba began to shake, completely out of control. She was taking large gulps of air, but she could not breathe in enough oxygen. Her brain and lungs were screaming out, burning.

"What on earth is happening?" asked Molly in her usual excitable way.

"Ssshhhh! Arthur!" whispered Ebba in Molly's ear. "He came to my room, and he tried to—you know. Thankfully, he was drunk and I managed to escape him. It's not the first time either," she confessed.

"Get into my bed," said Molly;" You can bunk up with me tonight. Don't fret. I'll look after you."

"Molly, don't you tell a soul! Do you hear me? If word gets out, I will be banished from this house, and I will have no place to stay. Mrs McAlistair is doing Jessica a favour giving me food and lodging. Please keep it a secret. Promise."

Molly smiled kindly.

"Promise! I mean it!"

"Alright. I promise. Now, calm down. Let's give it a while, and I'll sneak over to your room and make sure he's gone."

Ten minutes later, a terrified Ebba watched a cheerful Molly leave on her reconnaissance mission, her heart in her mouth. When the door creaked open again, she had a fright.

"It's alright, he's gone," reassured Molly.

She climbed under the covers with Ebba. Slowly, she started to feel better. Ebba was an educated woman, and she knew that she was going to have a problem with Arthur. She had a very short time left to live under the same roof as him. He and Betty were supposed to be looking for a flat. However, she knew his type from the slum. Men like him never stopped until they got their way. The days were going to tick by painfully slowly.

25

BUNKING UP WITH MOLLY

Ebba was so terrified of Arthur coming to her room that she began sleeping in Molly's room permanently. In the very early hours of the morning, she would hear knocking on her door to her room, and she knew it was him. The staff knew of Arthur's ways. It had all happened before, and they conspired to tell him that Ebba was at the hospital when he enquired about her. Ebba tried to stay away from the house as much as possible. She would sleep on an empty bed in the staff quarters of the ward, under the auspices of watching a very ill patient, or go to study in the hospital library instead of in her room.

A few days after Christmas, a frustrated Arthur summoned Ebba to the McAlistair's private library. He sent the message via Mr Carrington. Ebba couldn't refuse for fear of letting the cat out of the bag.

"Do you wish me to remain in the corridor outside the library, Ebba?" asked the butler kindly.

"Yes, please," she replied, terrified.

It was obvious that the old butler had suspicions about Arthur's motives, which thankfully he kept close to his chest.

The McAlistairs' library was an enormous room with books stacked right up to the high stuccoed ceiling. The bay windows were dressed with floral drapes, accompanied by swags and frilly decorative jabots. The walnut writing desk was French polished so professionally that the sheen had the clarity of a mirror.

Arthur sat in an easy chair, swirling a huge glass of cognac in a brandy balloon glass. He represented the perfect image of a gentleman, wearing a pin-striped suit. His shoes were polished to a patent shine, likely worked upon by a poor shoe shiner who did not have enough money to eat a meal that night. These days, he had chosen to hide his pretty boyish features, which had proved to be popular with the ladies but not so popular in the manly professional world. Somehow, the mature male clientele lacked confidence in his smooth dandy face, and he had more success hiding behind a grizzled beard.

"Please sit down, Ebba."

Arthur offered her a chair.

"No, thank you, Sir. I prefer to stand."

"Now, about the other evening, I am very glad that you are discreet, and haven't shared our little secret with anybody."

Ebba turned around and began walking toward the door.

"Sheehan," he said softly but wickedly "is not a very common name, is it?"

She stopped, and turned around to look at him.

"I believe that Sheehan is an Irish surname."

Ebba did not reply.

"What was your father's name, Ebba?" asked Arthur, with a sinister smile that implied he knew full well what the answer was.

Ebba remained silent.

"Answer me, dammit! What was his name?"

He walked up to her, and roughly pushed her against the shelving at the far side, away from the door to the corridor and the eavesdropping butler. Pulling her dress up once more, he ran his insistent hand along the bare flesh of her thigh.

"You had better answer me, Ebba!" he threatened as his hand worked its way up higher still.

"Elijah! Elijah Sheehan!" she shrieked.

Trying and failing to slap his hand away, she no longer cared if everyone in the townhouse knew and she had to sleep in the gutter. She had lived on the street before and she had survived. Arthur clamped his other hand over her mouth to silence her.

"No more shouting, do you hear me, or—"

She nodded, fear evident in her eyes, which he loved to see.

"I knew that I was right the moment I heard the name."

"I am not ashamed of who I am," she said, her body trembling with anger and fear.

"There are two things I'd like you to focus that powerful brain of yours on, Ebba. Firstly, if mother finds out about the conviction she will evict you. You were lucky my parents lead busy lives and did not read about it in the paper. You are the daughter of a murderer, and I don't need to remind you that it is not socially acceptable for a respected family like the McAlistairs to associate with your sort. We don't want you to become an embarrassing fascination when people visit us. Secondly, I doubt that the Salvation Army medical corps and the general committee will take kindly to having the daughter of a cold-blooded killer working for their reputable institution."

Ebba could not believe what she was hearing.

"So, in future when I visit you at night, you will invite me in, and be happy to see me. Do we understand each other?"

Ebba was speechless. Her whole career that she had worked so hard for lay shattered before her because she was the daughter of Elijah Sheehan, the murderer, and the only way to salvage it looked like becoming Arthur McAlistair's extra-marital plaything— to be picked up or tossed aside at his whim—a terrifying thought.

Mr Carrington kept his promise to stand close to the door. The only words he heard clearly were Elijah Sheehan. There was something familiar about the name, of course. He remembered it clearly. He was the chap that had murdered the tycoon Clifford Iverson's wife, Camilla. *Oh, my sainted aunt, what a social upheaval that had caused.* Mr Carrington had been a butler for many years, and he had a clear understanding of the politics of the upper classes. He knew that Ebba was undergoing some form of lustful nightmare inflicted by Arthur McAlistair throwing his status around, so he applied years of experience and delicately knocked on the door.

"Who is it?" shouted Arthur in an irritated tone, dropping Ebba's skirt at the sound of the knock.

"The butler, Sir," replied Carrington.

"I have a message for you, Sir."

"Come in man! I don't have all day," shouted Arthur.

"Sir, there is a man at the front door asking for you. He is not prepared to give me a note, and he insists upon speaking to you. Something about a case you are working on, Sir."

"Oh, bloody hell, why now of all times," Arthur cursed. "Ebba don't forget our conversation. Both of you are dismissed."

Arthur marched to the entrance hall and opened the door. There was nobody outside. He walked down the steps onto the street and looked up, and down. He could see no one. He went back inside, highly annoyed.

"Carrington!" he screamed. "There is nobody at the door."

"Oh, my word!" said the butler. "I assure you there was a gentleman caller. Can you believe that somebody could be so rude? Entirely unacceptable. If the vagabond returns, I will give him a piece of my mind."

Arthur waved his hand in dismissal. He did not give the stranger another thought. He knew that he had Ebba just where he wanted her. After thumping his way up the impressive family staircase to his suite, he shut the door behind him, eager for some privacy.

Betty had waited for her husband in their small sitting room. Their suite consisted of four large rooms, decorated to Mrs McAlistair's taste. The curtains and wallpaper were dated. The brocade upholstery on the furniture was very much of yesteryear. Everything in their accommodation reflected the fussy Victorian style of over-furnished rooms. The more modern trends in décor were moving toward lighter and brighter colours with less curtaining at the windows. According to Betty, people these days craved well-lit spaces, an antidote to the gloom so predominant in the more traditional nineteenth-century homes.

"Arthur, you know the flat we discussed?"

"Mmm."

"I have found something beautifully modern and light. It would be just perfect for us," said Betty enthusiastically.

"It is beautifully furnished although I would rather choose my own décor," she continued, doing her best to sell the idea to her husband.

"How much will it cost?"

"Well, I must say, it seems quite a bargain for the area. It only has a five thousand pound asking price, my love," said Betty in her most manipulative voice.

"Where is it?" asked Arthur.

"Don't you remember? I told you I was looking for places in Mayfair? This has beautiful marble floors in the entrance hall, and the rest of the floors are Burmese teak, immaculately polished. Do you want to look at it? It overlooks the most beautiful square from the balcony. We enjoy that on many a lovely summer's days." she continued.

"Yes, that sounds like the perfect exclusive address at which we can impress our friends."

"Would you like to see it?" asked Betty delighted that he had been so easy to convince.

"No, thank you, my angel. I trust your judgement entirely."

Betty was overjoyed. *Thank goodness he had said yes, or I would be living in my mother-in-law's stuffy old place forever.*

In the days after Ebba's grim experience in the library at the hand of Arthur, she found several successful ways to avoid him. Unfortunately, she did not know what her future held with the medical corps. It was undeniable that Arthur held a lot of power over a lot of people, and he would use it to crush those who disobeyed his forthright orders.

"Mr Arthur must have an enemy somewhere," said Molly one night. "He is an obnoxious excuse of a man, and there will certainly be someone who feels aggrieved."

"Molly, we are not powerful enough to take him on. We don't move in the circles of the rich and famous. Who would listen to us?"

"Ebba, you cannot continue sneaking around like this. Surely, someone with authority will speak up on your behalf?"

"Come now, Molly, you, and I have both been raised on the streets. You know how the upper crust gentlemen work. At their high-and-mighty jobs on weekdays, praying in church on a Sunday—and in Spitalfields brothels every night."

"I know. I know. And Her Majesty, Queen Victoria, monarch and sovereign head of the Church of England turns a blind eye to the abuse of the lower classes. Women and children, boys and girls alike. Nobody is safe from their libidos. Their money can buy anything—and it does."

"I have worked hard to become a doctor so that I can help people, and Arthur seems intent to ruin that unless I surrender to his stomach-churning demands."

"Perhaps you should tell Elliot?" suggested Molly.

"No!" protested Ebba. "He will surely kill Arthur if he finds out he's been making unwanted advances. Elliot is very protective of me. One murderer in my immediate circle is enough, I assure you," she added with black humour.

Back downstairs, it was Betty's turn to force her will on her husband.

"Darling," said Betty in her sweet but self-interested voice. "We will be moving to our new home soon. Of course, I have hired the most wonderful company to decorate and furnish the entire flat. It's an absolute steal at two thousand pounds for their bespoke service."

"That is perfect, my darling. I hope that you are enjoying yourself."

The hen-pecked husband felt staying on the right side of Betty was crucial since she was so well connected. Her social influence extended as far as the aristocracy, and members of government. She knew the prime minister well enough to be acknowledged in public by him.

Arthur didn't really have the money to spare for the flat or the decorating, but if he refused, he knew that he would face the wrath of her father. He had to marshal all his resources, call in all his debts, and get some hand-outs from friends to cover the outlay. He had just managed to pay the five-thousand pound asking price for the flat in Mayfair. Negotiating the price down had been fraught and in the end, Arthur had given up. The seller wanted to remain anonymous, and the transaction was done through a trust fund based in New York.

Obviously, it had been owned by a very wealthy American, which explained the modernity of the flat. The Yanks had a very different sense of style to the British, but it did not bother him. It was a refreshing change and would make the right impression, were he to host dinner parties or hold private consultations at home. He wasn't quite sure why a 'light-and-airy' place would need a further two thousand pounds to make it even more 'light-and-airy', but kept his mouth shut. If he picked up a couple more sizeable clients, he would be able to settle the redecorating account. *Hopefully.*

He had received the deed of sale, and as a prestigious lawyer, he was happy with the acquisition. He had not seen the property first-hand, but he knew Betty had spectacular taste. That was one of the few uses he had for his wife in his life.

"Arthur, my father will be in town on Thursday. They are still removing the previous owner's furniture, but he wants to see the flat nonetheless. Please attend. He will be so impressed with you and the home you have provided for us."

"Of course, my angel. I will be there. Perhaps, we should take a bottle of French Champagne and have a little toast to celebrate?"

Betty gave a small whoop of delight at the idea and flung her arms around Arthur's neck, an embrace he quickly wriggled out of.

Thursday afternoon arrived. It was crisp but clear and perfect for Betty, father James, and husband Arthur to see how bright the flat was. They walked along the corridor, sidling from one side to the other, dodging a flurry of activity as workers carried furniture to-and-fro, on their way to the servant's entrance.

Arthur was impressed from the moment they walked through the double doors into the entrance hall. The marble floor created a sophisticated first impression. He walked through the rooms. The servants' quarters were in a separate building behind the flats, linked to the main building by an underground tunnel. He liked that concept. His philandering would not be as risky. James Carmichael was also delighted with everything he saw.

Arthur had brought three tall champagne flutes with him in a picnic hamper full of alcohol and devoid of food. He popped the cork with a flourish in the sitting room. Lacking a proper table, he popped the glasses on the window sill, pouring the bubbly golden liquid into each crystal flute.

"Sorry, guv," a workman interrupted. "We just need to roll up the carpets, and get them out of here."

"Not a problem at all my man, please continue," said Arthur jovially, bursting with pride as he surveyed his new abode.

One at a time they started to roll up the oriental carpets and carry them out. Normally he would have snapped at the interruption, but that day, Arthur was enjoying imagining how jaw-droppingly beautiful his new home would be once the decorating and furnishing was complete. It appealed to the very heart of his shallow soul.

The last carpet was being rolled up. It was a beautiful large turquoise oriental rug, truly exceptional, and likely very pricey. *I wondered if I would look cheap if I asked to purchase it from that fellow. Probably. I really would rather not take the risk, I suppose.*

As the carpet was being rolled, Arthur noticed that it had covered a large stain on the highly-polished Burmese teak floor. The mark had noticeably absorbed into the wood. It was oblong, and he guessed it covered three feet by two.

"What on earth is this mark?" he shouted at the worker, his charm dissipating when he saw the unsightly spot on his very expensive, otherwise impeccable floor. "Get someone in here, and sort it out at once!" he demanded.

"Guv, that stain is not going to come out. You are going to have to lift the floor. We've had every decent polisher on our books through here, and nobody can shift it. Won't be cheap either. But it will be worth it."

"Well, what the hell is it?" yelled Arthur. "Please not a damp problem!"

Betty was getting embarrassed in front of her father. James did not like shouting and screaming. He deemed it 'common'.

"It's—well—it's blood, guv."

"What did you say?" asked Arthur frowning, not sure if he heard correctly.

"It's blood, guv. Didn't they tell you? This is the flat where Camilla Iverson was murdered by Elijah Sheehan. That's why a sumptuous Mayfair pad like this was so che—affordable."

Arthur frowned, desperately trying to quieten his mind. He was having difficulty accepting what he had just learned. In the meantime, he glared at Betty.

With her stress-levels soaring, his wife started wailing like a child having a tantrum before bed.

"I am not living here," she sobbed and ran out of the room, with her father following close behind.

"You remember Elijah Sheehan, guv, t'was that Irishman who had the affair with Mrs—"

The workman didn't have time to finish the sentence.

"Shut up! Shut up!" Arthur screamed. "Of course I know who Elijah Sheehan was! I am a blasted lawyer!"

Arthur was in a state of fury. He had spent money that he could ill afford for a flat that was the infamous scene of a violent society murder. He would never be able to shift the flat. Nobody in London would touch it with a barge pole. Betty would refuse to live there, and her father would agree with her decision. There would be hell to pay. James was sure to blame his son-in-law as the master of the house. But the worst thing by far for Arthur was the humiliation of it all. The joke was on him.

Back at Mrs McAlistair's, Ebba returned from her late-night shift at the hospital. It was a bittersweet evening. She could no longer keep Bess confined, her arm had fully healed. She had done her best to give the kind woman the rest she needed, after years of hard work.

"We will surely see each other again, Miss Ebba," said Bess, her voice tinged with sadness.

"Of course," replied Ebba. "I visit the coffin house at least once a month. I will stop by for some tea."

The two women hugged each other. Ebba returned to the ward to check on her next patient, and Bess left the hospital in good spirits. She waited on the pavement for an omnibus that would take her back to her humble home, itching to tell her girls more of her news.

27

TROUBLE IN THE SCULLERY

After another night shift, Ebba entered through the kitchen door. She was hungry but far too tired to make something to eat. She opened the bread bin and cut a thick slice from a fresh loaf, then gave it a good buttering. Nibbling on the snack as she crossed the floor, she navigated her way around the huge wooden table in the middle of the room. The moonlight filtered through the windows casting long shadows, and she did not need a lamp to light her way. She headed toward the servant's staircase, using the handrail to pull herself along, providing relief to her aching feet. As she began to ascend the second flight of stairs, she saw a man sitting in the shadows. Without needing to see his face, she knew it was Arthur McAlistair.

She turned around and ran back down the stairs as fast as she could. Unfortunately for Ebba, he was sober this time, and able to run much faster than her. The fabric of her long dress was tripping her up, and slowing her pace. She lifted her skirts a little and dashed across the scullery, but he caught up.

"You!" he screamed at her. "You and your feckless excuse of a father have ruined my life."

Ebba made an attempt to calm him like she had before, but it was futile. Arthur was enraged, and in that state, Ebba knew that he was capable of anything. She was in grave danger.

Ebba tried to say something to placate him.

"Shut up, you harpy!" he shouted.

With that, he hit her so hard about the head that she flew backwards landing on the table behind her. She felt dizzied by the blow, and her vision was blurring. She knew that she was going to faint with the pain. She tried to sit up, but he hit her again, this time it was with such force that she lost consciousness for what she presumed was a minute or two. In that time, Arthur set to work with his fists to make sure she was out cold. *I'll pummel every inch of her loathsome body.* When she came round, Ebba was in agony. Through the pain, she could sense her dress was hoisted up around her waist, her bare legs feeling the cool night air, the bunched-up material lightly pressing down on her belly. She looked at her attacker and saw his trousers were lowered.

"Every time you eat at this table in future, you little menace, Sheehan, you will remember me."

He growled, his nauseating voice the cruellest it had ever been.

She knew that she had to get up. He made a fist and hit her hard in the stomach again. Winded, she struggled for breath. Arthur was gearing up for another punch when they both heard the footsteps approaching.

Ebba could just see somebody was standing behind Arthur.

The moonlight shone directly on her, and she was illuminated like a heavenly vision. In her semi-conscious state, Ebba was convinced she was dead, and that it was an angel stood before her.

"Excuse me, Mr McAlistair, but what are you doing in my kitchen at this hour?" demanded Mrs Shaw in an ice-cold tone.

Ebba was too dazed to stand but was able to sit up on the table. Arthur spun around to see who it was, at the same time, pulling up his trousers.

"We have been seeing each other for some time," protested Arthur to the housekeeper, keen to explain away his clearly violent physical advances.

"I suggest you button up your trousers, Mr McAlistair, and leave my kitchen."

Arthur could not leave fast enough. His head was a mess. His life was falling apart, and interfering members of his mother's household had protected Ebba from his carnal desires yet again. His fury was driven by two things. Firstly, there was his manic obsession with exerting his passionate will over her. Secondly, his rage was driven by vengeance. He would surely kill her next time. A clever man of the law like him could hatch out the perfect scheme.

Mrs Shaw helped Ebba off the table. Her ears were still ringing from the cranial blows. Her mouth was bleeding, and her one eye was so swollen, already, she could not see through it. The ever-professional head of the McAlistair household took full control of the situation.

"Can you climb the stairs?" she asked Ebba.

"I think so."

Every step was sheer agony, so they ascended the stairs together, one step at a time. Once they reached the top floor, they approached Molly's door, and Mrs Shaw knocked on it.

A groggy Molly greeted them. On seeing the two women in front of her, she became instantly alert.

"How long has this business with Mr Arthur been happening?" asked Mrs Shaw.

"He's been threatening her since the night she went to dinner with the family—that night she was ill. She wasn't really ill, Mrs Shaw, she was trying to escape Arthur. He was taking advantage of her at the dinner table as everyone was distracted by Betty and Elliot's argument. And there was another time he made unwanted advances in the library. Mr Carrington had to step in to rescue her. You can ask him," explained Molly.

"Has he—mmm—" It was difficult for Mrs Shaw to say the words, but it was enough of a clue for Molly to understand.

"No ma'am. She has escaped every time. She sleeps in my room at night, and when he asks where she is, we always tell him that she is at the hospital."

"Why did you not come to me Molly, you know that I would have listened to Ebba."

"She was ashamed ma'am, and she was afraid to lose her lodging. But even worse he threatened that he would ensure that the trustees on the medical board would reject her as a doctor. He said he would let all and sundry know her father Elijah murdered that socialite, Mrs Iverson. He said he would make it his business to ruin her if she didn't comply with his physical demands. Luckily, she managed to avoid that fate—just."

"Molly run Ebba a bath, and see she is comfortable, please? Fetch her some tea. In the morning, I will bring up some breakfast. I want you to stay with her for the day. I'll say you're ill and adjust the rota. I don't want anybody through this door, do you understand?"

The situation was solved on a Sunday afternoon in a manner that no one would ever have guessed.

With the years of experience as senior servants, the butler and housekeeper had developed their own powerful network by mixing with other high society domestics. It was remarkable how much these silent servants knew about their masters and mistresses.

They were trained to be ghosts in the houses where they worked, and they practised being invisible so well that their employees often forgot that they were there.

Mrs Shaw donned her finest matching twin-set and coordinated hat, aiming to look even more smart and efficient than usual. She told the staff that she was taking the afternoon off.

Even in these extreme circumstances, Mr Carrington made a mental note of how extraordinarily attractive she was out of her employer's uniform.

Her plan was not out of the ordinary. It was quite common for housekeepers to call upon each other in times of need. The occupation of housekeeper was a highly responsible and respected position. Of course, the more affluent the employer was, the more highly prized the employee. Their communication oiled the behind the scenes wheels of polite society.

Mrs Shaw navigated the streets to the home of Richard and Rose McAlistair. Mrs Lessing, their housekeeper, was an old friend. They had worked together as maids in their younger years, and their friendship was still as strong as ever. She went to the servants' entrance and rang the doorbell. A short figure made its way to the door, then a distorted face peered through the single, bulbous, bull's eye pane. The blurred eyes within, seeing a lone woman, opened the door.

"Hello, Matilda," said Mrs Shaw, "I thought I could stop in for a quick cup of tea while I was in the area."

"Blimey, Elizabeth! What on God's green earth are you doing at my door on a Sunday afternoon?"

Mrs Shaw smiled. Matilda knew her too well to believe that it was an impromptu visit for a cup of char and a chinwag.

"Come into my office, Elizabeth. Let's go and talk privately. The walls have ears, as you know." She said loudly, as she heard footsteps carrying their owners back to where they were supposed to be working.

Matilda filled a teapot. The two women went into the office and closed the door firmly behind them. The housekeeper's desk was covered with ledger books and invoices. The wooden cabinets were all labelled by their function. There were no windows in the room, and it could become a bit stuffy with the door closed.

"Right, Elizabeth. Spill the beans, my friend. This is clearly not a social call." Matilda deduced correctly.

"You're right. I knew you would guess my motive."

Mrs Shaw related the story of Ebba and Arthur to Matilda, who listened without saying a word. There had been talk of the elder McAlistair boy's wandering eye and callous demeanour amongst their little circle.

"Oh, Elizabeth, you know this puts your job on the line as well," said Matilda solemnly as Elizabeth nodded.

"How are things for you here?"

"Good. Mr McAlistair—Richard—is an absolute gentleman. Rose is so good to us too. We work in a very happy household. You see, Rose doesn't come from a wealthy family. Her father is a highly-successful country vet, with many large, lucrative contracts with livestock owners up north—a self-made man you might say. That has made her far easier going than the rest of the aristocratic crowd."

Mrs Shaw hoped her jealousy was not showing on her face as Matilda continued. How she longed for a more harmonious household to manage.

"What we need to do is have this conversation in a place where Richard can hear it. It is the only way to get the story out. I am sure he will be livid when he hears about Arthur's shenanigans."

"But where?"

"Richard has a study, and next to it is a room where we file all the accounting documents from the kitchen. There is an air vent high in the wall, and you can hear everything that is discussed in the study. If we can hear him, he will hear us."

"Why would I be with you in the filing room?" asked Mrs Shaw.

"Because you are querying a bill that you believe was sent to the wrong Mr McAlistair."

"Oh, Matilda! You are an absolute genius. I simply knew that you would have a cunning plan."

"You know that for all his charm, old George McAlistair did the same things that Arthur is doing?"

"No!" said Mrs Shaw, shocked.

"Yes, I heard Richard telling Rose. It was confirmed by Mrs Atwood, who works for the Burrell family. That is why there was such huge staff turnover back in the day. Anyway, enough of that for now, Elizabeth. Let us go, and find that purchase requisition."

Richard McAlistair was used to the staff going in and out of the storeroom next to his study. He often heard them nattering away, but he was a reasonable man, and it didn't bother him as long as the chores he tasked them with were done on time.

He heard the door squeak open, and then he heard Matilda's voice speaking to someone, muttering away about a McAlistair invoice. Then he recognised the voice of Mrs Shaw. He deduced that a bill had been sent to the wrong household again, something that happened regularly.

Richard stayed sitting with his feet up on his desk, as he did some research for a case he was busy with. He wasn't aware of concentrating or eavesdropping on their conversation until he heard the curious words 'severely beaten'. It seemed it related to a tale Mrs Shaw was telling Matilda, the story of an event that took place at his mother's house the night before. Richard walked over to the vent, inquisitive about which staff member was responsible for the rumpus.

"Yes, Matilda. I had to rescue Ebba in the kitchen. Arthur had beaten her eyes shut, and she was unconscious on the kitchen table when I found her."

Did she really say Arthur then? Is he up to his old tricks again and getting handy with his fists?

"Heaven knows what might have happened if I had not arrived to help when I did. I don't know how to say it, Matilda, but Arthur had his trousers down around his knees. Dear God, if I had not walked in—well—"

Richard's eyes widened.

"Arthur was naked from the waist down, Matilda. I am so afraid he will dismiss me."

"Oh, Elizabeth, I don't know what to do to help."

"He has been tormenting the girl for months, while his wife is lying under the same roof. But worst of all he has threatened to ruin her reputation with the Medical Trustees Board for refusing his advances."

Richard was paralysed with indecision. He felt he owed loyalty to his brother, plus, he had only met Ebba a few times. However, Rose had told him what a lovely girl she was. Elliot had also taken a shine to her, and he was due to arrive from America that evening. He had written to Richard begging him to keep it a secret because he wanted to surprise Ebba.

Richard knew all about Arthur's strange tastes. He had believed that after his marriage to Betty, it would all stop. He was dismayed to discover that was not the case. Feeling disappointed and strangely responsible for the girl's welfare, Richard had to do something for her.

Richard walked into Matilda's office.

"Mrs Shaw. Mrs Lessing." He acknowledged the two women.

They both went to stand up, but he indicated for them to stay where they were.

"I heard your conversation ladies, and I suppose that was the intention. We all know about the vent in the study."

Neither woman said a word.

"I will speak to my wife. Ebba can lodge with us. Mrs Lessing, please prepare a room for her. May I ask that Molly accompanies her, if that is acceptable to you, Mrs Shaw?"

"In the servants' quarters?" asked Mrs Lessing.

"No, in the guest room, and put Molly in the room next door to that."

Matilda nodded.

"Mrs Shaw, please have Ebba packed, and ready to leave the family house by seven o'clock this evening. I will fetch her in my cab. How bad are her injuries?" he asked.

"She looks awful. She remains in good spirits outwardly of course, but we believe she is badly shaken. The repeated threats to her person and her professional reputation after all that hard work have taken quite a toll on her constitution," replied Mrs Shaw.

Richard shook his head in dismay about his shameful brother's conduct.

"Elliot is arriving tonight," he said. "There is going to be hell to pay."

"Please ask Dr Chadwick to contain his temper, Mr McAlistair. Ebba is severely traumatised. You will understand when you see her," warned Mrs Shaw.

"You should have come to me sooner," said Richard.

"I wish I had known sooner, Sir. It would have saved that child a lot of pain. She kept it to herself for a very long time."

Ebba edged herself down the stairs one step at a time. Mrs Shaw had insisted that Mr Carrington despatch the staff to their quarters so that nobody could see how badly Arthur had beaten her.

Richard had parked the cab in the courtyard so that she did not have to leave through the front door. He had always been a gentle soul. Even as an associate in his father's firm, he did not display the same aggression in his career as his father, and his brother. He was usually appointed to look after executing wills and property conveyancing, rather than cut-throat commercial matters and other forms of more aggressive litigation.

He strode through the kitchen of his parent's townhouse, slammed through the doors into the main hall, and went to find his mother in the drawing room.

"Mother, please come with me."

Mrs McAlistair shifted in her chair uncomfortably, annoyed at her son's unannounced arrival.

"Mother" he snapped. "I need to show you somebody in the kitchen. Please come with me."

Mrs McAlistair put down her teacup gracefully and stood up.

"It'd better be very important, Richard. And please consider your tone of voice when you speak to me in future."

She followed him into the beautiful hallway that had so impressed Ebba on her first day at the great house, then into a narrow corridor through to the kitchen.

Only three other people were present—Mrs Shaw, Molly and Ebba.

The battered and bruised girl was holding on to Mrs Shaw's arm, and moving very slowly toward the servants' entrance, every inch of her flesh aching.

"Richard, what is happening here?" his mother asked. She walked towards Ebba who, on hearing the angry footsteps, turned around to look at her. The girl's face was swollen and a nasty shade of red and purple from the bruising.

Mrs McAlistair put her hand to her mouth to stifle a cry. She'd seen it all before when George had terrorised some of their maids in the past. It was clearly not 'behind them'.

"Oh, God, no! Not this brutal violence under my roof again?"

Ebba kept lolloping awkwardly towards the cab. Molly helped her onto the step.

"I will look after her, Mrs Shaw. She will be safe in my home," advised Richard in a soothing tone.

The housekeeper nodded and went back inside. Richard was filled with disgust.

"Aren't you going to ask who did it?" he sneered at his mother, looking on as the battered girl sat herself down, wincing.

"Oh, Richard. I already know who did this. It was Arthur."

Richard stood aghast.

"You knew?"

"No, Richard, I assumed. He has clearly followed in your father's footsteps."

"My father?"

"Yes, Richard," she snapped. "There are many things children never know about their parent's marriages."

He looked at her in confusion.

"This is neither the time nor place to discuss it, Richard. Take Ebba to your home. You and Rose must look after her to the best of your ability."

Richard climbed into the cab with Molly and Ebba. Mrs Shaw stood at the window and waved a tearful goodbye. A stony-faced Mrs McAlistair withdrew to the parlour.

28

THE SAVIOUR
RETURNS

Elliot Chadwick arrived at Richard's home close to midnight. His butler had retired for the night, and the man of the house opened the front door himself.

Richard McAlistair's home was spacious but not as grand as his mother's or as magnificent as the flat Arthur boasted about. It had a warm, inviting feel to it, which reflected Richard and Rose's welcoming and relaxed personalities.

The house had the atmosphere of being lived in: books galore, comfortable settees, cheerful wallpaper. Colourful artworks gave the home an eclectic tone. It was one of Elliot's favourite places to visit.

"Thanks for having me, old chap," Elliot winked at Richard as he helped him with his trunk.

"I'll take it up to the guest room while you pour us a drink," said Elliot, parched after the long journey, keen to unwind with his friend.

"No, Elliot. Just leave it there for a moment. We—need to talk first."

Richard seemed particularly sombre.

"What's the problem, Richie. You look like somebody has died," smiled Elliot.

Richard did not smile back. He poured two large drinks and gave one to his visitor.

"Elliot, there is no easy way to say this, so I am just going to tell it like it is."

Elliot's cheery expression faded, a strange sense of doom filling the air.

"Ebba is staying with us. She is up in the spare room. Last night, my brother thought he would force himself upon her. When she refused, he beat her so severely she passed out. He was just about to have his way with her on the kitchen table when Mrs Shaw caught them. Goodness only knows what might have happened had she not stumbled upon them."

Elliot wasn't sure that he heard correctly. He was thankful when Richard continued to furnish more details.

"We found out that he has been terrorising her since the dinner you last attended with the family, when she ran off so early. It seems she was trying to escape Arthur's advances. Mother knows. I am not sure if it has reached Betty or father yet. Molly has come here too, to look after Ebba, and provide company when we cannot be with her. Apparently, she's been sleeping in Molly's room for quite some time to protect herself from Arthur."

Richard paused, seeing Elliot's troubled and confused look. They both took big swigs of their drink.

"She can stay here indefinitely. It's the least I can do to atone for my brother's evil behaviour. That offer extends to you too, Elliot. I just want to help her."

Richard couldn't meet Elliot's gaze. He had never felt so ashamed of his family in his life.

Sensing the tale was over, Elliot sank the rest of his drink, placed his glass calmly on the table, then charged up the staircase, two steps at a time. He did not knock, but opened the guest room door quietly, and went in. Molly was asleep on a chair next to Ebba. He touched Molly's shoulder.

"Go to bed and get some rest. You'll need all your strength for tomorrow," he whispered. "I'll take over from here—Oh—and Molly—thank you."

"Oh, and I am so glad you are here, Doctor Chadwick," she added, poking her head round the door before heading off to her own room.

Elliot tiptoed over to the other side of the bed, not wanting to wake Ebba. He stood and looked at her in the lamplight. He could not believe what he was seeing. The beautiful, cheerful face had taken a severe beating, and her left eye was swollen and closed. Her mouth and lips were cut where her teeth had smashed into her flesh. He looked at the blue marks on her arms. He didn't see the bruises on her legs, and thighs or the blackened patch on her stomach. It was a miracle that she suffered no internal bleeding.

Exhausted from the long and rough sea passage, Elliot climbed on the bed next to her and lay as close to her as he dared. He propped his head upon his elbow and watched her breathe. *I did not rescue you so that some thug could do this to you. I am never going to leave you at risk again. I'll protect you to my dying day.* With his sleeve, he wiped his tears away before they could betray him by dripping down his face. He kept a vigil over her for the rest of the night.

Ebba woke up before sunrise. She opened her one good eye. She could feel Molly beside her. She had to get up to use the water closet, but she needed help. With bleary vision, she reached out for Molly but got a terrible fright. There was a man next to her. She screamed in terror.

"Don't be afraid, Ebba. It's me, Elliot, and I've come to take care of you," he said in a soothing tone.

It was as if every ounce of Ebba's reserve crumbled. The years of having to look independent and self-reliant melted away. She began to weep, no longer needing to seem strong. There was somebody else to be strong for her. She felt his powerful arms envelop her.

"Shhh," he breathed softly. "I am here for you, and I will never let you be harmed ever again."

Having arranged hot water for a bath, he carried her to it like he had carried her when she was a frozen little girl. He left her alone to bathe, but despite trying desperately, she found it too difficult to undress. Tenderly, professionally, lovingly he helped her. Then he scooped her up and put her into the hot soapy water. He saw the bruises on her body, and it filled him with pity. He washed her as gently as he could, then dressed her, and carried her back to bed.

Ebba couldn't smile for two reasons. Her swollen and cut mouth was stiff and unmoveable. Worse, her heart and soul were also broken. She was bereft. Had it not been for Molly's constant companionship at night, she would likely have ended her life.

"Thank you," she whispered as he stroked her hair gently for a few minutes to soothe her.

"How many times do I need to rescue you, my love?" he murmured in her ear, but she did not hear him—she was already asleep.

He crept off the bed and went to sit on a rather rickety and uncomfortable bedside chair. He was just in time. Molly tiptoed into the room and whispered:

"Hello, Dr Chadwick."

"Come, Molly. Let's go make some tea in the kitchen. I need to know a few things."

Molly answered all Elliot's questions to the best of her ability.

She filled him in on the whole story from the night that Ebba had fled from the family dinner, Arthur's numerous unwanted advances, Molly having to share her room as a safe haven, and Ebba making excuses to be out of the house as much as possible. She concluded with Mrs Shaw's rescue of her on the table.

"Mr McAlistair—Richard—offered her a place to stay for now," added Molly.

"I know and I am grateful for that. But I am never going to leave Ebba alone with this family again. I trust my friend Richard, but as long as she is in the vicinity, Arthur will surely try and harm her again. Mrs Shaw may have agreed Ebba will stay with Richard until she is better, but I am marrying her, and taking her to Wales.

Far away from London, this miserable, stinking hole that has been so cruel to her."

He said it with resolve and determination. Molly was delighted and stunned by his revelatory news.

"Molly, will you come with us, not as a servant but as a friend?"

"Me?"

"Well do you see another, Molly? We'll need help setting up the practice and running it." he smiled.

"Yes, of course, I will. I would love to."

With some pressing errands needing his attention, Elliot left Richard's house. He would not be back until much later in the day. That night he had an invite to dinner at Mrs McAlistair's house and, if he were honest, he was not looking forward to the prospect.

The butler answered the door.

"Good evening, Mr Carrington,"

"Evening, Doctor Chadwick. The family are already in the dining room, but it will be my pleasure to interrupt them. I think you're just in time."

Indeed, I am, Mr Carrington. The butler opened the doors to the dining room without knocking. Elliot strode into the room to the amazement of everybody—except Mrs McAlistair. She was surprised that it had taken Dr Chadwick so long to get there.

Arthur and his father stood up and walked over to shake Elliot's hand in greeting, but the young doctor ignored them, using the opportunity to take George's seat at the head of the table. George McAlistair remained stood where he was, astounded by the invasion. Arthur skulked back to his seat, with a distinct inkling as to which direction the conversation might turn.

Betty stared at Elliot with disdain. Once again, the uncouth fellow had breached etiquette. She sensed her husband seemed a little edgy. Only Mrs McAlistair seemed calm, and indifferent to the situation around her.

"Good evening, Dr Chadwick—Elliot," she said kindly, "I have been expecting you."

"You have?" added Betty, her curiosity piqued.

"Oh, yes," confirmed Mrs McAlistair, looking directly at Betty. We have another guest arriving as well. Your father will also be here shortly."

"Daddy?" Betty asked, looking even more perplexed.

"Yes, my dear. Your father."

The door opened, and Carrington showed Betty's father, James Carmichael into the room. His daughter jumped up and ran to embrace him.

"Oh, Daddy! What a surprise to see you," she gushed, while Arthur looked on, rolling his eyes.

"Oh, my word, Mary! What are all these people doing here?" demanded George McAlistair, his concern increasing minute by minute.

"George, please be quiet," Mary said firmly, verging on rude. "Doctor Chadwick has a story to tell, and I agree that we should listen to it. Elliot, please go ahead."

"Why do I have to hear this story?" asked James Carmichael. "Is it about blasted miners' lungs again? I am tired of debating—"

Elliot cut into the conversation and nipped Carmichael's griping in the bud.

"—no, it is not about the miners, but rest assured we will have that discussion in the future. It is about Arthur, your daughter's husband. Because, frankly, James, after you have listened to me, you will need to take her home with you." warned Elliot in an ominous tone.

"Two nights ago, Betty's dear husband Arthur beat Ebba Sheehan severely and tried to rape her in this very house. It was witnessed by two of the staff who thankfully stepped in to stop him."

He had made the statement. He had put the truth out there, and now he was waiting to see where the chips fell.

"Oh, please, Elliot. I am a married man," sniggered Arthur. "What would I be doing seeking pleasure with such a lowly girl. It's a preposterous suggestion."

Undeterred by Arthur's blustering denial, Elliot continued.

"He beat her so severely that she can barely walk or see out of her eyes."

Betty looked confused. James Carmichael, who prided himself on being a good judge of character, was studying his son-in-law very closely.

"Oh, this is probably all a great misunderstanding," said George McAlistair.

The door crashed open again, and Elliot, along with everyone else was surprised to see Richard there.

"No, it's not, Father. I had to come and fetch the girl. She is staying with Rose and Molly while she recuperates. And what Elliot says is true. Arthur beat Ebba to a pulp yesterday. She can hardly walk or talk, and she cannot see out of her one eye."

Arthur stood up and started to pace the room.

"What are they talking about, Arthur?" asked Betty.

"The girl has been pursuing me endlessly. I didn't want to upset you, since she lived under this roof. I had to fend her off, once and for all. Words were not enough."

"There we go then," said George, keen to turn the conversation away from Arthur's conduct, and by implication his own in the past. "It is all just a jolly old misunderstanding, isn't it? Let's all cheer up, and have a round of drinks."

"Father, perhaps you will be less exuberant to brush the matter aside if you were to know that one of your staff found Ebba unconscious on the table, her skirt hiked up, and Arthur standing over her with his trousers around his knees." chastised Richard.

"Truly Richard that is the crudest accusation," snarled George McAlistair, his jolly tone gone. "We don't discuss things like that in our house. Especi—"

"—is it true?" Betty interrupted, glaring at Richard.

"Don't listen to him, Betty. He has always been jealous of me." growled Arthur, now circling the room like a defensive caged animal not wanting to be poked and prodded by its keeper.

"Stop!" commanded James Carmichael, the loud outburst making everyone's head turn to look at him. "Come on, man. Answer my daughter's question. Is this true?"

"Of course not. It's complete balderdash. A jealous slur on my character and nothing more," said Arthur unable to look his father-in-law in the eye.

Mary McAlistair sat serenely as chaos ensued around her.

"Admit it, Arthur, damn you!" yelled Richard.

"Arthur, what have you done? Richard seems to be very earnest with his allegation. Daddy, please do something!" cried Betty, finally igniting the simmering fury in Arthur.

"Oh, shut your trap, Betty. I am so sick of listening to you. Always wanting something. Trying to be better than the Jones's. Looking for the perfect life. Well, let me tell you, you can stop searching. It doesn't exist. You are portraying the girl to be some sort of saint. Well, you're wrong. All of you. Do you know who Ebba Sheehan is?" he screamed. "She is the daughter of the murderer Elijah Sheehan, and her mother was a whore on the streets of Whitechapel, and you doubt me, your own husband? She asked for it. She literally begged for it. She would not leave me alone, so I took up her offer, and the little cow changed her mind, yes. She deserved to get a good beating. She asked for it. She is a common whore like her dead, alcoholic mother."

Elliot stood up so fast that he knocked the heavy wooden dining room chair over. It took him two steps to reach Arthur. He grabbed him by the throat and began to choke him. Arthur's face was turning blue, and his tongue was sticking out as he gasped for air. Richard pulled Elliot off him, roaring:

"Stop! Elliot! You are going to kill him. Enough!"

Elliot quickly tore himself away from Richard and grabbed Arthur by his hair. The fiend was still disoriented, and with all his strength, Elliot drove Arthur's head against the wall, again, and again. Richard fought to restrain him, but Elliot was like an unstoppable machine. When the red mist cleared, and Elliot came to his senses, the suffocating bloodied mess of Arthur McAlistair lay in front of him. For the first time in his life, Elliot Chadwick had no compassion for the injured human in front of him, his Hippocratic oath cast aside. It was the only time in his life that he genuinely wanted somebody to die.

The room was in chaos. Betty was crying. Carmichael was in a rage. Richard was calming Elliot.

"Dr Chadwick! This is totally unacceptable under my roof. How could this terrible behaviour occur in my home?" screamed George McAlistair.

Amid all of the activity, Mary McAlistair stood up and began to speak in the most dignified manner. The moment was surreal.

"Don't you dare ask that question, George! Terrible behaviour has always occurred under your roof. For years you sexually abused our staff. That is why we could not keep them long. Then you would come to our bedroom, and physically abuse me. I spent so many years worrying about what society thought that I wasted my whole life staying with a philandering wife beater. It is time for this to stop, George. I will not let one more innocent girl be victimised under my roof. I am also divorcing you, George. Living with lawyers for years has sharpened my own legal axe. I will defend myself with the evidence I have of your dalliances. I know of many an ex-employee who will testify on my behalf. If you get any ideas to contest the divorce, I will make sure that every sordid detail of yours and Arthur's behaviour is emblazoned in the newspapers. Attitudes to domestic abuse are changing, George. It is no longer something swept under the carpet."

George was about to take her to task about her comments, but the deathly stare he got from his estranged wife, persuaded him otherwise. *I should deflect attention onto Arthur.*

"As for you, Arthur, you should be charged and face the courts."

Arthur was sitting on the floor with his back against the wall, blood flowing onto his shirt from the head wounds Elliot had inflicted upon him. He stared at her, his own mother, with pure hatred as she continued.

"But, I'm no fool. I know you and your father are thick as thieves with every crooked judge in this country. I will have it arranged for you to work overseas. You will be going off to Johannesburg in South Africa. You will stay with one of my associates. He only has sons and no daughters," she added. "I don't care what you do there, Arthur but I never want to see you again."

"I can't go there," screamed Arthur. "It's a hell hole."

"Yes, Arthur, it is. I would prefer if it were a grave, but for now, a hell hole is good enough."

Richard and Elliot left the house, leaving the bitter scenes behind them. Mr Carrington and Mrs Shaw were given instructions to help Betty and Mary McAlistair pack for a few nights in a hotel. James was to accompany Betty. No one was keen for them to stay with Richard or

George. Everyone had seen enough of the seedy underbelly of the two, vile McAlistair men and wanted to be free of them for good.

Leaving the cab, the two men walked in silence to Richard's house.

"Thank you, Richard," whispered Elliot. He wanted to say more, but he struggled to speak without getting emotional.

Elliot climbed the stairs to Ebba's bedroom. He lay on the bed next to her and protectively put his arm over her while she slept. If Arthur tried to seek retribution in the night, he would have another fight on his hands. Eventually, his overactive mind let him get some much-needed rest. It was only broken when Ebba sat up in the morning. He looked at her and smiled as her one good eye fluttered open.

"Elliot" she whispered.

"You are beautiful," he confided, as he kissed her gently on her forehead.

"And so are you, inside and out," she whispered.

"How many more times am I going to have to rescue you, Ebba?" He spoke tenderly at first, then followed the words with a cheeky grin.

"Don't make me laugh, Elliot. It hurts."

29

THE BLACK VELVET BAG

Despite several months of planning, Elliot, and Ebba's wedding was not the usual kind attended by distant aunts and uncles whom the couple hardly knew. They were formally married in the Salvation Army Citadel, and afterwards, they had a small reception at Richard's house.

At first, Elliot was hesitant about having the reception there. So much had happened and he wanted the perfect day for Ebba, but she had convinced him not to worry about making bold, extravagant gestures. She won him over with simple facts.

"Well, Elliot, it's either, Richard's house or the coffin house—because those are the two safest places that I have ever known."

Rose McAlistair went to a lot of trouble. The garden was beautifully decorated for the event. Even the sun made an effort, shining from morning till night.

Their wedding was attended by a very different set to those normally found at a marriage of the rich and famous. As Ebba walked down the aisle of the Citadel church, she saw all the faces who had nurtured her, and for whom she had cared for in return. Mother and father of the groom, Jess and John Chadwick, Suzanna, Mrs Shaw, Mr Carrington, Walter, fellow students, and lecturers, and of course Mary McAlistair made up a few of the fifty people that they invited.

Bess Grantham and her daughters arrived with husbands and children in tow. Sadly, Ebba found out good old Mrs Thomas had died a few weeks beforehand when her daughter politely declined the invitation.

Molly was the bridesmaid. She yelled when Ebba asked her:

"Who would have thought I would be a bridesmaid for fancy people."

"It's Elliot and me, you fool. What a ridiculous comment!" laughed Ebba. "Fancy people, indeed."

Ebba wore a plain white dress with white lace over it. Her hair was loose, and her short veil was held on her head by a simple silver coronet, adorned with white-scented roses rather than glittering diamonds.

They exchanged vows, and Elliot put her wedding ring on her finger. The guests cheered when he kissed the bride. The newly-wed groom gave a sheepish look out towards the congregation.

When the wedding party made it to the garden reception, the mood was jolly. There was a string quartet playing chamber music which drifted into the open air, floating on the wind.

"Are you happy, Son?" asked John.

"Yes, Pa. I love that woman with all my heart," Elliot replied, beaming.

He looked over with delight to see Ebba with his mother, chatting away, tongues wagging like washerwomen, before his face turned rather serious.

"Father, you are a Godly man. Answer this for me—"

He paused, ashamed of the topic that was burdening him.

"—When I found out what he had done, I almost killed Arthur McAlistair. Should I have forgiven him?"

"My son," advised John, "let the matter go, and don't feel guilt or shame over your actions. In my faith, we are taught to forgive. But when it comes to my family, deep down in my soul, I

always believe in an eye for an eye and a tooth
for a tooth is the only answer when carefully
chosen words have failed."

Elliot and Ebba spent the first night of their honeymoon
at the Regency Hotel in London. Now both fully-
qualified, nothing was keeping them in the capital. The
next day they would take a train to Wales, and go in
search of their first home.

As they undressed each other in the glow of the
crackling, orange firelight, Elliot was in wonderment of
the beautiful body that he was touching. All the scars
had healed. She was flawless. The passion of their love-
making exceeded all expectations for a first time.

Her hair rippled over the pillow, and she gazed at him in
adoration, he was so dashing. He held her close, and she
could feel the warmth of his body and the beat of his
strong heart, a heart beating for her and her alone.

The relief of knowing she had a dependable, honest and
capable man to protect her was indescribable. After
such a tough start to life, the knowledge that she would
never be cold, hungry or hurt again was nothing short of
a miracle.

Afterwards, he propped up his head on his hand and
smiled down at her, lovingly.

"I am so glad I found you, Ebba."

"Are you always going to look after me?"

"Always."

"Are you always going to save me?"

"Every time you need saving, I will be there."

She laughed. It was their secret little game. She always asked the same questions, and he always gave her the same answers.

"I have a gift for you," she whispered, before reaching for a small velvet bag on the nightstand.

"What is it?" he asked, intrigued.

The tiny velvet drawstring bag had his name embroidered on it.

"Your mother helped me with it, bless her. You have to promise me that you will always keep it with you." She whispered wiping tears from her eyes.

"Why?"

"It's an outstanding debt. Promise me!" she demanded, clasping her fingers around the bag to hide it from view.

"Alright! I promise," he chuckled, which despite the levity of his delivery, was another solemn commitment to his new wife.

Elliot pulled the drawstring and slowly opened the bag. He tipped the contents out, curious to see what they could be then looked down to see what he was holding.

He was overcome by emotion, for in the palm of his hand, lay the same four pennies he had given his mother for his new wife's lodgings, all those years ago.

Printed in Great Britain
by Amazon

17168316R00160